SIMPLE MACHINES

Manuel Carreon and Marla Dean

Slaughter House Press
Austin, Texas

Published in the United States by Slaughter House Press

Slaughter House Press and **SHP** are registered trademarks

ISBN: 978-0-692-26682-3

SIMPLE MACHINES
Slaughter House Press LLC
www.SlaughterHousePress.net

Printed in the United States

Cover Design by Kerry Ellis

To Simone

Acknowledgements

I write this with the deepest regard for the fighting men of 1st Battalion of the 75th Ranger Regiment. My time among your ranks is a badge of honor which I am proud to wear each day.

For Rangers past, present, and future who gladly lay their lives on the line every day for our great country, I am indebted to you. Let us all never forget those who paid the ultimate price and will never return home. Toast to their memory and celebrate the life of a true warrior.

Rangers lead the way!
Manuel Carreon, 2014

Special thanks to friends who have read various drafts, supplied their much needed feedback, and given their endless support, especially, Rosalyn Rosen, Del Weightman, Drew Julian, and Norman McCallum.

CHAPTER ONE

Breathe deep. Burning diesel fuel and its black smoke mixes with the smell of a nearby bakery and I awaken to this place. The odors trigger years of memories with flashbulb images of the history we created together. Like the indigenous people that toil outside this base I am tied to the Afghan land and let the smells fill my lungs, washing away any lingering fog of my former self. For the first time in almost six months, my dormant identity starts to claw its way to the surface of my being. The familiar sound of gravel under my boots accompanies me just as it always has. In a rhythmic cadence I become less of what the world I left behind recognized and more of the man required in a combat zone. My beloved combat zone...

The sun becomes a brilliant red as it fends off the night. On the horizon are the mountains, old friends, reminding me of their presence as they glow and fade into the dusky heavens. Beyond my orders, my duty as a Ranger, Green Beret, Delta Force Operator, or whatever boots I have volunteered to wear, it is the mountains which have left their marks on me and I carry their scars secretly as an appreciated gift. These ragged masses represent my time in this place and are a testament to my strength, memories, and accomplishments and must be treated with the appropriate reverence. My boot prints may fade, but this place will swallow my blood and hold memory. As I take these first pulsing steps, I can feel the land's thirst.

Moving from the cargo jet I'm quickly consumed by the landscape. I can feel the heat of turbine engines burning me as they wind down in preparation to refuel before the long return to the States. I savor the dual sensation of the warmth on my back and the cool Afghani sunset on my face. As the jet engines die and my back slowly cools I become whole. Soon there will be no wasting time, no more duality, or the tug of my personal life and the messes I have made;

no more assigned titles, like ex-husband, drunk, or son. This is the moment when it begins, the first steps where I become more of what I believe myself to be. My name is Master Sergeant Joseph Cevera, and I am a man with the simple purpose of a soldier and the tools and desire to go to war.

I look back to the C-17 and see my squad of operators breaking free from their cocoon. I count seventeen men in all as they stretch their wings and fight off the haze of downers taken to pass the flight. Instinctively, all of them follow me from the cargo plane in silence, and I slow my pace allowing the men to scan surroundings, gain bearings, and move into their new world. Awake and alive at last, they experience their first taste of the possibilities of this place and its foreign familiarity. For now, they move like ghosts lamenting a past life, but these moments like mine are fading. They are trained and capable men who share the same desires as me. As they gain distance from the plane, they too begin the transformation of the butterfly. Without the pettiness of the world and beyond materialism that plagues the earth, or greed that brought us into this war, they are simply men looking to me and waiting instructions. These soldiers are nothing more than a collective purpose soon to be brought to life on the battlefield. They are the most beautiful sight I have ever seen. I turn my back and walk ahead, knowing they are behind me and secure that I will guide them. Each man is an experienced veteran with a personality as individual as their fingerprints. Each has left his mark on this land and knows where we are going, but none would step ahead of me. Leading these men is the reward for my years of service and it is a role I cherish. Too soon we will journey together to the very edge of this world and the very limits of ourselves, and I have no doubt that each man will continue to follow me with unrelenting obedience fortified by blood and sacrifice. This is our way. As their soft shadows appear behind me, I can almost feel our united heart beats. We are becoming one consciousness, one beast, readying its self for what lies ahead.

We load into the waiting shuttles as the excitement grows. Many years have passed since conflict became my life, and many faces have come and gone. The war makes all encounters brief and intense. Often, all that remains are the memories. I think of men I haven't seen in years and wonder who will be waiting for us at the hanger. So many ties form during our work and due to the secrecy in which we all exist these threads are often left hanging and frayed. Seeing a familiar face allows their story to continue and gives everyone hope instead of the obvious alternative that war has to offer. Pulling off the tarmac, I'm on the edge of my seat anticipating our family reunion.

The shuttle bobs and weaves along the runway, filled with familiar sounds of jokes and sarcasm, but I am quiet as our overcrowded transport clumsily enters a hanger. The first of many smiles appear on our faces as we see the group waiting for us; everyone begins to cheer and call out names in excitement. Some of my men jump out of the shuttle before it comes to a complete stop causing the driver to swerve, but his confusion is drowned out by the noise of handshakes, hugs and laughter echoing off the galvanized walls. For a brief moment there is no tomorrow, only the gratitude from the embrace of a long gone friend and the joy it brings. We come together and for this instant time has stopped. Everyone picks up exactly where they left off with their brothers. Inside jokes resurface requiring no explanation, stories are retold to a familiar cast, and my men are welcomed home to their life and work. I watch as my family enjoys each other and sit back to receive the second gift of the evening.

Several minutes later, a flatbed truck roars away with my men sitting in the back on mounds of gear, jovially chatting away with their blood brothers. The rest of the boys are sent on various errands, leaving me alone to walk to the compound that Special Operation Units call home. I turn and take a last look at the maze of runways that brought us into this place and watch as the evening wind moves waves of dust across my view. Clenching my jaw, I hear the grains of sand grind against my teeth. I've only been on the ground for a short while and am already becoming one with the land. Everything is in its place.

Leaving the airstrip and turning onto the main road of Bagram Airfield, the sounds and bustle of city life surround me and devour my view of the horizon. The site contains everything I just left back in the States. Soldiers prowl carelessly on the promenade, stopping only to offer a half salute to the occasional passing officer. These are people making the best of their situation and taking a much needed break from the war that dominates every facet of their lives. Everyone here, from the mechanic with the oil stained shirt waiting in line for a latte to the cook lounging at the Burger King enjoying food that he didn't prepare, are clawing out a moment of peace in this world. Coffee shops are filled with groups of men eye fucking women, who bathe themselves in the attention, and the Burger King has a line of fat brass also scanning for potential subordinates they can fuck. Despite being in a war zone, no one seems to have any place to be or anywhere important to go. I see uniforms faded from months of sun and worn from weapons slung across backs. Tucked under shirts everywhere are weapons carried as though they are invisible.

Moving along this sea of camouflage and bloused boots, I keep a quick pace and stare at the ground six feet in front of my toes. I don't bother offering a salute or making eye contact with anyone. These people are all off duty and have no need of military courtesies. Besides, in this place I am a man without rank or name. My unit has no patches for me to don on my shoulder or banners to fly. My civilian clothes, beard, and the Glock pistol that hangs on my hip offer enough detail to my identity that soldiers in my vicinity instinctively and reverently move out of my way.

Off the crowded street I slide into the shadows of an alley and move hidden in the dark corners, walking parallel to the bustling street. I'm accompanied by nothing but the sound of my boots crushing gravel and the rough stone of the outermost wall sliding past my fingertips. I know each step as if I'm walking through my own house at night. The stones guide me through the darkest parts of my path. During their attempt to rule the Soviets built this wall. It has endured decades of abuse and still stands waiting patiently to house the next batch of invaders. The alley comes to a sharp right hand turn signaling my first stop of the evening. For a moment I allow my eyes to focus before stepping onto the porch of a crudely constructed shack. I hear a television buzzing inside and a heated debate in *Pashto*. I try to pick out words of the native language before following custom and letting myself into the house.

A dozen, young, Afghani men are glued to a television watching a rerun of *Dallas*. In their grey and tan robes, they are like mushrooms as they squat on the ground far too close to the screen. Two of them look in my direction, while the others continue to debate the show in their native tongue. The men who see me immediately erupt into smiles and jump over their group. Engulfed with hugs and handshakes my reunion continues. They are the interpreters or "terps" as we call them, and are the eyes and ears of every operation that takes place in this huge military installation.

One of the young men darts into the back of the house and returns with a box. Cradling the package like a baby he timidly offers it to me. It's as if I was expected. I'm always amazed, they seem to know who is coming and going and are usually more aware of schedules and operations than anyone on the base. I chuckle at the box in front of me and pull out my own offering from my backpack. The room falls quiet as every eye focuses on the present. Slowly their delicate hands tear open the package while I put my gift away. The first layer of tape disappears and the group cheers and laughs discovering their new treasures: three full seasons of *Baywatch* wrapped in a poster from *Knight Rider* and two Harry Potter books.

The interpreters immediately revert to the young boys that they are and surround the gifts acting as though it's Christmas morning. Some of them I've known through most of their lives. They are the bastards of this occupation somehow collected along the way and now serve for the remainder of the war. Even though they are free to go and are paid a salary for their service, it is simply too dangerous for them to leave. Seen as traitors by their culture, they will be the first victims when the U.S. pulls out. It is the price of their servitude.

After small talk and promises of more gifts to come, a young man named Petch walks with me as I leave the house. We instinctively stay away from well-travelled paths and move through a series of turns and alleys until we are beyond the noise of the main street. Petch and I walk in silence as stillness returns and my mind begins to slow to a comfortable focus. Meanwhile, the sun lost behind the earth allows the night to cool everything she touches. I hear the shivers in my friend's voice and listen closely to everything that has happened in the past few months.

Battling the chill of the night, he rushes the conversation in hope that he can soon return to his warm house and the gifts I brought. When given the opportunity, he, like most of the people I've come to know in the Muslim world, is a simple and honest man. I honor Petch by entrusting myself to him and he reciprocates by offering me his knowledge and interpretation of ongoing operations in the region. His intelligence concerning the war is better than any I'll receive from the agencies.

He talks of places I know well and the names of men I have hunted for years. The story he tells of my next 100 days paints a stark reality of the road ahead and once again I am thankful for my men and their abilities. Petch continues to speak with me in a soft whisper for a moment longer as we reach my final stop for the evening. I stand on the balls of my feet peering over one of the outermost walls and become hypnotized by the landscape outside the fortress. In the fading light of day rows of brightly painted red rocks warn people to stay away from the bordering minefield. The crimson columns seem to go on forever until lost to the night sky. In the distant darkness is a mountain and beyond the mountain is a war.

For now the thought of battle vanishes as the night air kisses the back of my neck and tickles the inside of my nose. I'm lost for a moment in the sight over the wall and Petch senses I've stopped listening. He disappears. Stillness overtakes me and I savor the moment for as long as I can until evening prayer echoes against the world outside the wall.

"Ash'hadu an laa ilaaha illaaah", a voice sings through the static filled loud speaker and I roughly translate his words to mean, *they bear no witness and there is no other God than Allah.* For the first time I feel a chill as the prayer invades the dark night. My reality suddenly returns and reminds me there is much to come. I attempt to shrug off the cold and back away from the crumbling wall, but the prayer still rings in my head even as details of work flood my thoughts.

I know in the coming days I will draw my weapon and take my men head first into the war that rages just beyond my view, but for now, the night still calls my name and asks me to savor the quiet. I feel the anxiety building and swell with the excitement of a first day cherry private. Too quickly, the last moments of peace evaporate and I willingly embrace my first night in the combat zone.

CHAPTER TWO

We have only been in country a few hours and most of the men begin to settle into their routines. These practices will pass the time and get them through the next 100 days in this place we now call home. Movies, books, and calls to the States are of little comfort to me. I prefer to organize, prepare, and plan. Over-preparation is my routine and the team knows to leave me alone during the first few days of a deployment. They understand after a few missions a gentler, kinder me will re-surface, but until then the boys steer clear of their boss. My mind races through the list of things that need to be done and the time restraint that accompanies each. I leave the men without a word in search of my new desk where I will spend the majority of my time while at base.

I am jolted by the noise of the Tactical Operation Command (TOC) as I enter and pick up my pace in the hope of not being seen as the new face in the room. Men are working, yelling into phones, and abusing keyboards. The commotion is reminiscent of the floor traders at the New York Stock Exchange, but unlike the sounds within the team house I welcome this chaos. Each man is filled with the purpose of an ongoing operation unfolding before them on a huge plasma screen mounted on the main wall. Every eye in the room is focused on the massive display and I take comfort that my arrival is totally unnoticed. My isolation is complete within the noise.

Down one of the aisles I find an open computer in the middle of the space. My desk consists of a table made of untreated 2X4s with a chair and dusty laptop. Forty-three unread messages are waiting. I scan the names from the senders and open an email from my boss entitled "Master Sergeant Cevera: Merry Christmas". The fact that my boss includes my rank implies sarcasm; we don't use such formalities in our unit and my curiosity is sparked. Interesting that I've forgotten Christmas is only two days away. The outside world has vanished very quickly.

After reading some bland work related updates, I open an attached video file. It begins with some opera-like music in *Pashto*. The voices sound like a choir, but unlike the church hymns I heard on holidays when dragged to Catholic mass by my mom. This music is filled with drum rolls and accompanied by a low hiss created by dubbing a tape over and over again. Similar to any number of pirate broadcasts that flood Middle Eastern television, the music is very militaristic and triumphant. The first image on the screen is a book flying in and opening.

Enter the Koran. Doves fly from the pages as a commanding voice reading a passage from the book overpowers the music. The voice eventually fades away as the music rises in volume. The image of the Koran abruptly cuts to black. I look over my shoulder to make sure that I am still invisible, but my attention snaps back to the computer by a blast of unrecognizable sounds and images. Leaning toward the screen, I struggle to decode the movement and sounds. It only takes a second before I realize I have seen this movie many times.

I make out the sounds of AK-47s firing in the distance and attempt to decipher the worst camera work I've ever seen. Someone shouts in Arabic as trees, ground, and a camera man's frantic feet blur together. The yelling continues and ends with a scream. I latch onto the noise and recognize the cry. It isn't the shriek of a Middle Easterner in agony, but the sound of an American shot in a very painful place. He must be wounded in the knee or the stomach. The cameraman stops running and focuses on the target, but the image is still unclear. The sound of the soldier falling to the ground in surrender pushes me to the edge of my seat as the footage continues.

I struggle to make the fallen American mean nothing more to me than a gunshot wound and I want him to die. It would be easier for him not to live in slow agony with the knowledge of horrendous torture that will quickly follow. I need to distance myself and yet, I watch on, clenching my jaw and sitting back. My mouse hovers over the pause button, but I allow the movie to play on, feeding me its horrid message. The screen cuts to black again leaving only the hiss and as a new scene appears I can feel its pull on me. Finally, the film reveals its purpose: bodies on the ground.

Two men lie next to each other and from the dirt covering them, I know the bodies were dragged for some distance and then staged for the camera and the world's entertainment. In order to tell the story of these deaths in detail all of the entry and exit wounds are highlighted. The cameraman, no longer running, slowly pans over every inch of the twisted bodies. Bullet holes still ooze a mixture of blood and dirt and organs can be seen through the larger openings of the shredded torsos. The camera zooms into the yellow discharge of open mouths and pans back to show the world that the dead are Americans. Their faces frozen in their last horrible moment are captured in a low pixilated resolution.

I catch myself looking down at the keyboard to shield my eyes from the images and force myself to look at their faces. I need to see them, not out of reverence, but as some sort of self-imposed punishment for averting my eyes. I am weak for turning away while my countrymen lie on the ground. I have seen hundreds of the dead and with each, revisit a reality that I've known since this war began. Death in combat does not look like a peaceful sleep and we all suffer to the end. This is the way it is and I need to get over any hint of regret or hesitation. All are things I should have left behind in the States. I give myself a moment to regroup and focus upon my surroundings.

The ongoing operation on the wall still holds all eyes in the room. This is war's pornography. Too quickly I'm drawn back into the staged broadcast on my screen. I understand it is the only victory for our enemies in this conflict. The masked men before me are heroes and saviors to their countrymen. Their world, the world we created through years of ill thought-out foreign policy, holds such a hatred for the United States that publicly displaying our brutalized dead is the only revenge possible. These images like the ones we show on CNN create solidarity. To kill a man, a stranger, a son, a son of America is the only triumph the Middle East will ever see until we can no longer stomach this war. I know this and still my eyes veer away from the screen. There can be no real victory here. There isn't any ground to be gained or lost, no flags to be flown, just this perpetual stalemate, a meat-grinder that continually feeds on young men and the poor. Dark thoughts and still I accept my station in this place.

With determination I return my gaze to the bodies on the ground and thank God for my abilities. In the midst of the room's chaos a familiar and welcome hatred grows inside of me. I let it bleed in and overwhelm futility and any regrets that linger. My trigger finger slowly caresses my chair's armrest and muscles tighten as I see myself standing over the bodies of those responsible for this film. I hate them for what they are and what they are about to do.

The most disturbing part of these videos is the stripping of the bodies. Every part of the uniform of a soldier is interchangeable, except for his weapon and his boots. A soldier cares deeply for both. I know without hesitation I can identify every man on my team by his boots. This symbol of a soldier contains his footprint on the earth and his past. When a man dies in the Special Operations community, more often than not, his body is left behind or hastily shipped to the States. Worn boots on a plain ammo box, a rifle stabbed into the ground, and Dog Tags hung on a trigger are the only memorial most of these men ever have. After a brief moment of silence is offered, a fallen teammate is quickly forgotten as the next mission approaches.

These parasites on the screen don't understand the true value of their new possessions. They simply steal honor from the dead and leave them to rot without dignity or history. These bodies, no longer human beings, are now symbols to exploit and place on stage. The humiliation of these soldiers equals the humiliation of America. I want to scream as the boots of the fallen are taken, but turn my emotions inward to be saved in the deepest most hidden part of myself for use at a more appropriate time.

The enemy like vermin scurries into the pockets of the dead and quickly empties them. I stare as the scavengers remove an identification card from one of the bodies. The soldier must have forgotten to leave it behind before his mission. I hear laughing as the living hover over the dead and the identification card is held up to the camera. A man speaks in heavily-accented English from behind the black sheet that wraps his face, "Matthews, Robert, United States Navy, Active Duty." I am completely caught off guard.

In my world, the Special Operations world, we live, work, and die in the shadows. I deployed with men for years that only knew me by my nick-name and I preferred to keep it that way. It is easier to keep everyone at a safe distance, even my friends, because in this reality relationships are all statistically short lived. To hear Robert's name gives him an un-welcome face and personal history. He now has a past, which includes tears and suffering over the loss of him. My safe distance, like Robert's boots, is stolen. Here is a young man staring at me with the fake smile he only used for photographs and probably the same smile on the wall of a suburban home where his parents live. No longer dehumanized, I look at a boy who was taken way too young and never got a chance to live the life he deserved. I pause the image and stare at the clean shaven baby face on the identification card. I wonder if he had a family of his own, bills, and all the other crap young soldiers acquire to feel like grown men and not the boys they actually are.

All of my team are young and volunteers. My boys are also fathers and husbands with thirteen children between them. Their lives are my concern for reasons other than the obvious task of keeping them alive and completing the mission. When a man is pulled from the team by the birth of a child, a divorce, or even if he dies, a gap is created that affects the entire unit. I wonder if my team might have to finish what the dead man in front of me has failed to do. I don't want to think about his wife or the possibility of him having children. No matter how I feel my emotions must always be secondary to the mission. This is necessary for my survival and my men.

The dead before me are Navy S.E.A.L.s and I heard about their patrol before arrival in country. The men before me could easily have been a team of Green Berets, another Delta group, or Rangers being paraded around on the screen, or even worse from my own unit. I begin to calm down, but am still unsettled by my sudden attachment to the men on the screen. It is much easier to think of dead SEALs as gaps to fill or as an objective that needs to be met rather than as men with families and dreams. My breathing grows easier as my focus shifts and I return to the film.

The masked enemy very carefully puts the American's identification card into his own pocket. It is a nice trophy and proof of his victory. I tell myself that all soldiers steal. Our enemies take boots, watches, and anything that might have value. Americans steal photos, money, and anything they can hide from Custom Agents. It is generally accepted that once a soldier is killed on the battlefield he is no longer a man, just pockets to go through for a souvenir or simply something to step over. The theft is a validation I tolerate. It is a confirmation for soldiers on both sides of a battle. These stolen objects from the dead are proof that the thieves have survived, but I've never grown comfortable touching the bodies. It feels wrong. Luckily, I've forgotten many of the faces and the trophies taken to confirm my own survival. There have been so many bodies that my history and memories are fused and faded.

Numbness blessedly returns as the camera pans back to the bodies. Abruptly, the scene cuts to another image of slaughter. A new soldier is shown on the ground in a fetal position. His hands are pulled tight into his chest as though he died in great pain. His body is riddled with bullet wounds. Those celebrating before the camera caught up to the man, stood over him, and emptied their weapons. His shirt is ripped apart exposing the remnant of a huge tattoo on his swollen belly. Once again, the camera creeps slowly over the body and pauses over each bullet hole. As the boots are pulled off, the body turns over, and the face of the man is fully visible, revealing skin hanging by blood clots and tendons. He was shot in the back of the head and the bullet exited through his chin. His face is clenched tight with the remainder of his teeth exposed. I wonder if he was a good looking man once, and now there isn't any way to tell.

He probably lived long enough to watch his friends die and then made a break to salvage his own life. It isn't enough that this man chose to leave his friends to survive. He is still paraded around as a trophy on Middle Eastern television. Angrily, I grip the table and focus on the wood, the floor, anything to get me out of this man's story. I am locked into his last moments. I think about myself in his place and of all the firefights and near missed bullets. My mind races through the many times I have made the decision to leave the fallen and the almost dead. I understand when a decision is made to live; it usually means that someone else will die.

This soldier chose to leave everything behind. He turned his back on all of the things that make a hero in our world and decided to ignore honor, refuse selflessness, and abandon his unit. He probably heard a shot, a scream or even a cry for help as he ran for his life down the mountain. For whatever reason, he wanted his life and it was more important to him than the pleas of his brothers dying behind him. His compensation was to die alone, in agony, looking up at the faces of the men who killed his team.

I know I am capable of making the same decision as the dead man and the least noble thing I have done in this war is to survive. My reward as a soldier is to live through six rotations in combat zones while carrying the suffocating weight of my choices and knowledge that every heroic action is accompanied with an element of hidden shame. Until my days end, I'll never know who got off easier in this place, the dead or the living. My numbness and distance are now completely gone. I see nothing but the images and the delivery of emotions.

Their team camped out for the day attempting to find roads for other military units to use. While they rested, a man and his son herding goats stumbled upon them. The SEALs had no choice but to let them go. The released pair ran to an Al-Qaeda hideout, reported the Americans position and the enemy returned in force. They were a team of twelve against thirty armed enemy. This is not like the action movies I loved so much when I was a kid. In this situation a bad outcome is certain. They were going to be slaughtered. I was told that they held out for four hours as they attempted to work their way down the mountain and escape. In the end, they were simply outnumbered. I reach into my shoulder pocket for a cigarette. I know I need to watch the video again, but I can't with the stories of dead men rattling in my brain. I barely hear the noise in the room anymore and wonder which one of my boys will be lost this trip and become a symbol of victory on Middle Eastern television. The future has yet to be told to all of us, me included. Like Vegas it is my training that increases the odds of our life span, but the cards are stacked against us. Life and death in this place are so random. War is random.

I put an unlit cigarette in my mouth and fish for a lighter. Merry fucking Christmas. I envy the men surrounding me, hurried in their repetitious routines, and without thought only purpose. Sitting low in my chair, I examine the scars across each of my knuckles and remember a time when my hands were clean and unmarked by the hundreds of teeth and blunt objects they have collided with; a time when the only possibility was glory, unlike now, where outcomes are often repugnant. The video on my computer is coming to an end and I feel my hunger for a new mission growing. I want to be unleashed. I am ready to contribute to the pulse of this room and go to war once again.

CHAPTER THREE

The mind is a funny thing. A smell, a sound, even the temperature can shift us back into a memory so clear. Within this small space of exhilaration, in a room full of madness, my mind races to escape. I walk out of the noise and try to remember the feeling of being young, trained, capable, and ready for war. The taste of that pure awakening is long forgotten and smothered by reality. In those days, before I had ever seen a Middle Easterner, or set foot overseas, I would stare at the ceiling at night and dream about where I am today. At one time, Ranger School and its ceremony were etched deeply in my thoughts as a beginning. Tonight, the overwhelming memory of knowing the sureness of my path is somehow seductive.

Outside the TOC, I smoke in relief, but my mind is a million miles away. The moments of certainty from my innocence appear ghostlike as I exhale into the cold night air of this place. The base surrounding me evaporates as the past invades. I close my eyes and see plumes of steam rising like the smoke stacks of Chernobyl from the ranks of young men where I once stood.

Collectively our body heat ascended and testified to the ticking bomb of nerves that had become my graduating class. Each man had survived their first real taste of hell. Ranger School was about to end. I can almost hear the slight echo from the loud speaker bouncing off the massive trees that enclosed the parade ground as the Sergeant Major droned on about honor and courage. The mere sight of us only whispered what we actually had endured. The ceremony had not lasted more than twenty minutes, but I had found it difficult to keep the shivering in my legs from becoming noticeable. I shook not because of the January morning but from the excitement that was building within me. During those 61 days and nights so much pain and suffering was swallowed and I thought nothing would ever be worse than Ranger training.

I feel myself attempting to bury the experience, but an image of my mother's face on that day appears, confused and searching. Somewhere in the crowd of gathering civilians on that day she sat waiting for her part in the ritual. She used to stare at me like I was a stranger, and I remember wondering if she would even be able to pick me out from the mass of worn men that stood with me. I entered the course weighing 255 pounds and by graduation was an emaciated 195. My pants clung to my hips with the aid of rope cut to serve as a belt. Newly exposed ribs, sunken cheeks, and dark circles under my eyes were the only badges I wore to prove I survived when others quit and buckled under the pressure. My class starting at 400 had dwindled to 30 capable men.

I remember feeling as close to the heavens as I had ever been while watching the incredible beauty of the sun rise almost 60 days in a row. I felt alive and thankful for the sensation. Men lost their minds out on the long nights during the course. It was the first time I questioned my ability to survive and succeed and I was not alone. I was among men who at that moment were working for nothing more than their own survival. It was this intimacy that forged our bonds. It drew us closer than our bloodlines or marriage vows. Eventually, we found the finish line and I came to a simple truth. If you have never pulled at the seams that hold you together, you have not lived. I stood with the remaining men on that frozen, January day and cherished them.

As the Ranger ritual ended, I picked up Mike, my mentor and buddy, over my head and began to walk towards the frozen pond that had been the backdrop for our graduation. I was invincible. I left my mother to stand alone and was sure that I had found a new home. I hear Mike's laughter in my ears as I reared back to throw him into the water. Out of my hands, I watched my friend flail through the air, comforted that my strength had never failed me and as his body broke through the thin layer of ice, I knew I would never stop until I had joined the ranks of the most elite unit I could find in this Army. It seems a hundred years ago when I dove head first into freezing water, collided in the air with several of my classmates, and felt the prick of a thousand needles rushing over my body. I was baptized into my new life that day.

Treading water and laughing, our relief and excitement surfaced in shivering giggles. My classmates hurried to climb out of the frozen pond while Mike and I lingered moments longer enjoying the cold. Mike was a Captain about to be Major in charge of a Special Forces Team and I had been invited to join his group as soon as I could be released from my Ranger Regiment. To me his cool was unfathomable; most of the ranking soldiers I had met were uptight automatons and the exact opposite of Mike's demeanor. It didn't matter if he was in the middle of a patrol in Iraq or in Ranger School; his confidence rendered him incapable of being rattled by the cadre and allowed him to breeze through any grueling situation. At all times he was a Hollywood star gliding the red carpet. Mike. . .

I pull out another cigarette and lean against the TOC wall in the shadows. I am invisible under the cold stars and with ghosts. Mike, my buddy, was killed in battle, leading and protecting, five years after that January morning ceremony. He is part of this place.

He was the man I wanted to be and I catch myself smiling, thinking of how hungry I once was for the next challenge. Strange to smile now, but nothing seemed unattainable then. I had already made up my mind before the ceremony ended that I would continue to push myself while in the Army. I once thought those first days would be my worst and now they seem like a welcome relief. I stifle a laugh at the gung ho geek I was and lean my aching back into the cold wall as thoughts of those days sweep over me. I hear Mike's laughter and look up at a half a billion stars.

The images of dying SEALS abruptly ends my relishing of the past and the sound of a distance jet loaded with meat for the beast brings me back to the reality of this war. I think of all the young men seeking their own victory and that first freezing breath and moment of exhilaration with Mike becomes a distant dream.

These remembrances of the dead are a weakness and steal from the living. There is a mission waiting and details to be formulated, men to be organized and readied. The video must have shaken me more than I thought. I should be concentrating on what is coming, talking to the boys and yet, the image of the cherry private me panting at the bit for this war is so clear. I sit in the dark and struggle to remain in the present, but I am weak and finally surrender letting the memories have their way with me. Seven years ago my love affair with this place began and as I open the gate to the past I am suddenly there.

The plane banked hard as the crew yelled we were landing in thirty seconds. The G-force pulled me deep into my seat and I half-expected artillery to narrowly miss the plane, but the C-17 found the ground without incident. I was almost disappointed when the back ramp opened and the only thing that assaulted me was the heat. Men started tearing off their jackets and sweaters which had protected them from the freezing cabin. I was a cherry private in the mortar platoon in 1st Ranger Battalion on my first deployment and had no idea that the plane was going to be so cold. I had frozen through the entire sixteen hour flight to Afghanistan. As the hot wind exploded against me I welcomed the Middle Eastern summer for the first and only time.

The soldiers meandering off the ramp looked more like they were strolling through a mall than stepping into a combat zone. Two long hours later our equipment and bags were dropped in front of our group. As the fork lift backed away I jumped on the pallet and began to break the straps as if it contained some great treasure. I worked quickly and still expected gunfire to start at any moment. I wanted to be prepared. The men moaned in chorus at the announcement we were "going out" in twelve hours. I smiled. My imagination ran wild with all the climactic moments of every action movie I'd ever seen. I was the first to put on my body armor. It felt cold against the sweat of my back and sent a chill of excitement through my body. I knew I was ready for anything the enemy could send my way.

Our convoy rolled out of Bagram Airfield heading first south and eventually east to the Pakistan Afghanistan border. The sharp, jagged, red mountains grew out of a dull sand desert and the dust found its way into every crevice and irritated my skin. I took it as a good sign that everything looked and felt familiar to my home town of El Paso in West Texas. We climbed in elevation. In the back of the hummer I watched the sun set three times before my feet touched the ground, but when we arrived at our destination I eagerly walked up the path to a shabby mud house. Even for this side of the world its condition was substandard, but it didn't matter to me. I was home.

The first month of my first deployment passed in the blink of an eye. Three weeks were spent digging shallow graves called fighting positions and filling sandbags. The only break from my shovel was guard duty which entailed a machine gun nest on the roof of the safe house and baking in the sun. I was eagerly waiting for an inevitable attack on our position, but as the weeks passed I continued to stare at the landscape and realized I hadn't even seen a local. I had nothing but my shovel, machine gun, and determination to keep me going. My mind was my only company and conversation. During the first days I made lists of the girls I fucked and the restaurants where I wanted to eat when I got home. I thought about anything to pass the time and kill the boredom. Nothing was what I expected it to be and I decided joining the Army was a mistake. As the weeks turned to months my imagination surrendered to the routine.

With only four hours of sleep a day, physical exhaustion soon set in and everyone turned into a drone. We were ants that never stopped. I didn't shower or shave, hadn't changed my socks in weeks, and slept in my boots and body armor. Each day I was awakened by a kick. I put on my glasses and stepped over the other men who slept on the floor fully dressed holding their M-4 rifles like teddy bears. There were no conversations so I forced food into my mouth out of habit and took the 143 steps required to climb out of my sleeping bag and onto the roof for my guard shift. This started the twenty hours of work ahead of me.

By the end of the first month the world outside of our safe house ceased to exist. I had memorized every bush and tree over the top barrel of my machine gun. I gazed at the same hill and little valley every day and felt like I had always been on the roof. In the beginning I heard random laughter or a conversation, but now there was only silence. My state reminded me of Ranger School and during my guard shift I imagined this type of exhaustion would be the same when I volunteered for the Special Forces Assessment and Selection course. Soon my memories of being a Green Beret in 5th Group faded as I realized I was losing chunks of time. Hallucinations from sleep deprivation were on their way and soon I wouldn't be able to stay awake while on guard. I began to do push-ups on my shift attempting to stay awake. When this wasn't enough to fight my growing urge to sleep, I made myself imagine the enemy coming down the hill. I would slide my eye into the sight and fix my barrel on some random bush and pretend to pull the trigger. Without music, books, and the addition of deadly repetition, pretending to kill became my only entertainment.

My day was broken up by Red, my boss. Every day I heard his footsteps approach me from behind and after a slight pause he would turn and leave the roof. If I was digging he would grab a shovel, dig with me for a moment and carve an X to mark where the next hole needed to be. Red tried to prepare me for my first deployment. In his raspy voice, he told me that I was the best rookie he had ever had and how I was going to do great things for the Army and the United States. I left the meeting with an extra spring in my step, but that day like my entire life had become a vague illusion. Holding my machine gun, I wondered what good I was doing in one of the most remote parts of Afghanistan. I wasn't told why we were here or how long we were going to stay. My deadness slowly was replaced with anger when I realized everyone had lied to me, even Mike.

This fury kept me alert and my frustration kept me awake. I began to hate everything. I hated the sight of the other men who worked next to me, and while on guard I despised the Army, and when digging I detested Red. After a period of time even rage took too much effort. My anger was long past when the goat herder appeared walking his sheep. He moved from the south and as he crested the hill I fixed my barrel on him. I hoped he would give me a reason to pull the trigger and break the monotony. Every other day he walked along the same path and I followed him through my sight. I fixed slightly ahead of him, allowed him to walk into my crosshairs, and then pretended to squeeze my trigger. I quickly shifted my weapon ahead of him and let him walk into my scope once again. I could kill him seven times before he disappeared behind the brush and as he vanished my crosshairs hovered where his torso might be. I pictured his body exploding as my machine gun cut him in half. I made myself shift and move my weapon with a sense of urgency because I was determined to be ready if he actually made a move.

He was a poor goat herder who had done nothing wrong, but I still fantasized about shooting him. One day he and his sons came to the safe house wearing the biggest smiles they could fake. They clutched onto bread-filled baskets and nervously repeated, "America Good, America Good." Our interpreter explained the offering was to keep us from shooting their goats. I was on the verge of madness. Seven weeks passed and I understood why prisons don't rehabilitate criminals. I had never been so completely deprived of stimulation and focused on nothing except murdering the innocent goat herder. I was addicted to the idea of killing and every time he disappeared from my crosshairs I felt the immediate symptoms of withdrawal.

Instead of eating my second meal of the day, I chose to sit on my sleeping bag and clean my rifle and pistol. I disassembled, reassembled and held my weapons in my hands savoring the feeling of the pistol grips. My M-4 always strapped to my back, sparkled like diamonds against the dirt floor and was part of me. I tucked in my shirt so that my 9mm was always visible. On guard, my eye never left the sight of my machine gun, a finger always on the trigger and my thumb tensely poised on the safety switch. It was a compulsion stronger than any I had ever felt and while awake my longing to kill became an actual physical pain.

"It's not going to be long now," Red said one afternoon as he watched me dig. I was startled and resented the sound of his foul mouth and wanted to punch the smile off his face. "I can always feel it coming," he continued as I jabbed my shovel into the earth in frustration. "Don't worry boy, it won't be long," he whispered as he jumped off the sand bags and walked off continuing to grin. Before this deployment Red was a man I admired and had worked tirelessly for his approval, but now he was nothing more than a liar. I returned my attention back to my hole and like any drug addict focused on what I didn't have.

The next day fifteen minutes into my shift on the roof I heard a gunshot. My mind raced as I decoded the foreign sound. In disbelief I heard more shots fired which in a weird way sounded like someone flicking a piece of paper. The men below were yelling and scurrying into their positions and I froze in fear as the shots increased into a full dialogue.

Amidst all the noise I couldn't make out anything. Men yelled at each other and I felt the air displaced as bullets rushed over my head, but I didn't move. Slowly I got control of myself and I leaned into my machine gun. I dropped my eye into the sight; my finger slid into the trigger well, and then felt a tug at my leg. It was Red who motioned for me to move to the side. We made eye contact and I knew he saw my fear. He motioned again and I relinquished my weapon. He crawled on his belly to the 240 Bravo machine gun and it screamed to life. His eyes opened wide as his whole body shook from the controlled bursts. I buried my head in my arms and attempted to shield myself from the shower of hot casings leaping from the smoking weapon. I was betrayed and Red had stolen my dream. My sole purpose was gone and I wanted to die as the steaming metal rained down upon me. I had failed.

Less than half an hour later the gun fire changed to erratic bursts and stopped. I lifted my head and scanned the hillside knowing that I never fired a shot. I had let my team down and was sure Red was going to fire me. How could I have ever thought I could make it in this type of world? I was weak. Red still posed behind my machine gun alive with his eyes wide and focused. He took shallow breaths through his mouth and I admired him once again because he had succeeded where I had not.

When my boss tensed and dropped his face into his weapon once again, I leaned forward and saw two men walking down the path of the goat herder as though they were undetected. Red pulled the trigger, but the machine gun jammed. He opened the weapon trying to revive his patient as I drew my M-4 from its position underneath me. Calmly, I took careful aim at the man walking in the lead. Never lifting his eyes from the machine gun, Red quietly said, "Kill the man in trail." I shifted my cross hair to the man in the rear. The past months had taught me every step of the goat path and I knew exactly where he was going. I took aim slightly ahead of him and watched as he tried to navigate through the rocks. I leaned into my weapon and switched it to FIRE. I held my half-breath and pulled the trigger.

There was the slightest delay. It was only a fraction of a moment between the time my rifle recoiled into my shoulder and the man's neck opened like a fire hose as he fell to the ground. "You get him?" Red asked in excitement.

"Yep," I answered trying to remain cool.

"Just wound the other one, I want to have a talk with him," he said looking through his sight to examine my work. Red's smile grew as the man continued to bleed and roll down the hill. I took aim at the other man who was watching his wounded partner in confusion, but this time placed my crosshair much lower. I was aware of everything around me and felt my boss' excitement. I knew I wouldn't miss as I pulled the trigger. The man buckled at the knees and crumbled to the earth. We watched through our sights as he rolled onto his back holding both hands at his groin. As my enemy rocked in agony, I calmly moved my crosshair to look at his face. My heart no longer raced and the terrible thirst was finally quenched. I was at peace. Red sent a team to recover the wounded soldier for questioning. It was over, but I continued to scan the goat path for more possibilities.

I had done the unthinkable. Stillness fell upon my body and my mind filled with the images of my life. I asked Red if he wanted me to help with the recovery. He smiled at me and said, "Your work is done for the day, get the 240 up." Red crawled out of the nest and I was alone again watching the writhing man on the path. The one I killed looked like a rag doll carelessly tossed on the ground. His eyes were open looking up at the sky. I studied every inch of his body. My crosshair swayed over the huge red stain on his robe. My weapon was a paint brush. I was proud of myself as the feeling of failure washed away and all the rage inside me forgotten. I felt fifty feet tall and in love for the first time.

About an hour after the fight another rookie showed up to take over my shift. I was confused by his early appearance, but was told to report to Red immediately. As I crawled off the roof I heard laughter and noticed the smell of cigarettes for the first time in almost a month. There was so much activity I hardly recognized the place. The house and the men were alive again and everyone looked refreshed and happy. I walked up to Red and cautiously announced my presence, but before I could finish he turned and smiled. "You did good today." Nodding in response, I nervously started back to the roof where I felt more comfortable. He stopped me and held two bullets and a cigarette in his open hand. "Come with me," he said as I took his offering, "You're gonna have a new schedule from here on out." I followed him around to the back of the house. I scanned the faces of all the men who stood guard and although I had lived and slept next to them for two months, they were all strangers to me. We turned a corner to find a group standing in a circle. In the center curled into a bloody ball of pain was the man I shot

I was surprised at how small he was as he rolled around begging for help. "Doctor, Doctor," the man moaned.

"No Doctor!" the Major yelled. "Not until you tell me where your friends are hiding." The Major was hovering over the bloody man with a look of disgust on his face. I wanted to tell everyone that the man on the ground was mine, my trophy, and leaned further into the crowd to get a better look at my work. I saw his intestines hanging out of his belly. His little hands were covered in blood as he tried to contain his organs.

"Water," the man gasped despite the pain. The Major emptied his water bottle on his face. The enemy choked and began to vomit violently and with every convulsion more blood and shit leaked out of the wound.

The Major questioned him again in a much colder voice, "Where are they hiding?"

I stood and watched in disbelief. I was in some dream world filled with horrors and was oddly comfortable. I lit the cigarette and savored the burn as the smoke entered my lungs. It was the first one I had smoked in over a year, but Red's cigarette tasted sweet. Most of the men also had cigarettes dangling from their mouths and like me had mud and food bits clinging to their beards. We all smelled like a mixture of sweat and shit. I stepped to the side to get a better look at the Major and touched the shoulders of a man on the other side of me. He pointed at my cigarette and I handed it to him. Small cracking pops filled the space between us as the tobacco burned from his drag. I found my place among the crowd and moved closer to this beautiful disaster. I felt like a god.

These feelings seem like something that happened to someone else. The chill of night invades the memories and my cigarette suddenly loses its appeal as the phantoms fade. There is no time for this, but my former self clings to me as I stand in the night attempting to shake off the past. I'm concerned about this break from reality and refuse to allow myself to wallow in this self-indulgence. Pushing away from the wall and its isolation, the demons and images scatter, replaced with details, time tables, responsibilities, and maybe even fear. "You gotta pay your dues, Cervera" . . . Mike's voice floats after me and suddenly I am cold to the bone.

CHAPTER FOUR

My head is a million miles away when the squirrely man stops talking and places his hands on his hips signifying a change of thought. "Are there any questions?" He smiles, pleased with his performance of the Army's new sexual harassment policy. Two days into the deployment and the Army's mindless bureaucratic face continues its torment. Luckily, I remain focused and cleared of debris. My strange and uncontrolled visit to the past seems only a momentary stutter and I am free of its confusion. I am fine and ready for this guy to shut up. These seminars are the last prick of the military's needle to remind us that we are still their property and must clear this last hoop before releasing us into combat. The briefs are mandatory for all Army personnel and somehow, despite being Special Operations soldiers, we still fall under this blanket mandate set by some bureaucrat that probably has no idea that we even exist.

The response to the little man and military poli-cy is a shuffle of chairs as my boys work to leave the room. The presenter stands in the front of us, hoping for some sort of validation for his time. His confident grin fades quickly when he realizes the moment will never come. I post at the door and smile at the line of rolling eyes and huffs each man expresses for the waste of his time. After the room clears my team leaders, Marty and Q, linger behind for instructions. "Load up." My words have an immediate effect. The two nod and walk out quickly to perform the errands they have eagerly awaited since our arrival. Like me, they only have a vague idea where we are going or what we will be doing when we get there.

High ranking brass are coming and going in the control room, and Trap, my boss, is lost in a sea of meetings without time to update me on the mission. The complete blackout means that gears are turning. There is something unknown hovering over us, tan-gible, thick, suffocating, and all the while the clock is ticking down to zero. Everyone is on board the same rollercoaster climbing the first big rise. Inch by inch, click by click the chains and cogs pull us skyward. We are almost to the top and over the end. The ground and track ahead are not visible, but still we move to the crest regardless of what comes next. No force including our will is able to stop the ride from roaring along its predetermined path. We are at the highest peak and see the landscape below as our car slows to almost a stop. There is only enough time to look around at those sitting next to me and brace myself for what is to come.

I am finally called to my Boss' office and surprised to see three of my fellow team leaders from my unit sitting at the conference table with their heads buried in stacks of paper. No one bothers to look up and acknowledge my arrival. The weight and responsibility placed before them makes common etiquette insignificant. The only sounds are Trap, my boss, jovially humming and the freight train rumble of the air conditioner as it works overtime to keep him comfortable. Taking my place among them I wait patiently. The man to my immediate left, Alex, closes his folder quietly and rubs his eyes. Under other circumstances we would be laughing about our paths crossing, but observing the vein throb in his forehead tells me this is obviously not the place. Alex pushes his folders away in defeat and I know this is the last time we will be together for the rest of the deployment. The only other conclusion to my relationship with the men in the room will be a random encounter along the way when paths cross or a picture on a wall in memorial.

Two pages emerge from Trap's safe and end up in front of me. "This is the highest priority," he announces to the room. The other team leaders for the first time look at me. Despite the friendships shared with everyone in the room, I feel the sting of their resentment. I am the child over-praised by his parents to the point of embarrassment. I consider the assignment an honor, but dread suffocates my pride at the moment. I turn over the pages and place the photo on top and burn the image into my brain. It is a subtle message Trap gives me and I know I am going to lose men. My boss is comfortable and grinning, but all I see are the images of dead SEALs.

Alex stands, breaking the tension in the room. Trap levels his gaze on him and asks, "Are you good?"

"No," Alex answers quickly and looks down on me. His eyes are calling for help, but instead my drinking buddy flashes a quick smile and quietly leaves the room. In this world, at this level, your duties are something you endure alone and matters of military codes prevent me from any type of interference. Turning back to the pages before me my thoughts linger on my friend. There isn't a farewell or even a hand shake, just an absence of energy in the space. One by one the other men leave the room with various expressions from despair to excitement and suddenly I am alone with Trap.

"Are you good?" his question breaks the long silence.

"No," I respond in honor of my friend.

Looking up, Trap rubs his bald head and ignores my response, "That one's a big one."

"I know, I recognize the face," I respond without emotion. It isn't the number **4** on the photograph, which signifies his order in priority within the terrorist organization, but his name buried in the page of information that seems familiar. Trap leans toward me from his chair and his smile widens waiting for me to acknowledge my mission. I give him nothing, fold the two pages into a small square, and shove them into my shoulder pocket. I can feel his irritation as he leaves me alone in the room.

The pages paint my target as a super villain responsible for the deaths of hundreds of military personnel, but like most of the war lords I encountered, he is simply a pawn looking for some sort of notoriety and status in his community. It would be dangerous to underestimate him. My objective is to find him and his sons and retrieve them for interrogation. The primary target has leprosy and hepatitis. Nature will handle him for us, but my orders involve his bloodline and legacy, both of which my boys are planning to take from number 4 in our violent fashion.

I write over a page of notes before Trap bursts back into the room, announces "tomorrow night," and quickly slams the door. My heart sinks and I try not to show it on my face. I gather my notes and listen to my boss' excited footsteps disappearing down the hall. I know I have a sleepless night ahead before boarding the helicopters, and still need to meet the pilots. I have no use for men that are decorated and ranked, who speak of the fight as a thing of the past. I have to make sure these additions to the team are similar to my men, hungry, upwardly mobile, and willing to sacrifice themselves for the objective.

I force myself to walk slowly and calmly the short distance to the command room. I want to scream, run, and roll on the ground, anything to relieve the tension as the death mask of the young Navy SEAL floats in my mind's eye. I feign deep thought as panic freezes any forward movement. Forty-eight hours ago I was in control, ready to command but now, I hesitate. I manage to portray myself as a man strolling on a beach, carefree and at peace. Mike would be proud. I grab my laptop, thumb drive, and feel the eyes of the room on me. No longer invisible the weight of their expectations are confirmed by my boss' thunderous laughter overtaking the room. I peel the American flag patch off my shoulder and shove it into my desk drawer along with my military I.D.

I step into my third sunset in this place and find Marti and Q waiting for me. A host of orders spill out of my mouth and for now any hesitation and lingering fear are buried beneath a sea of tasks. The mission is revealed and its resolution is simple in terms of war. Now is the time to focus, go over every detail, and leave no room for error and yet, I can't seem to fight the flood of the past. Trap's laugh rings in my ears and transports me to another mission and kill. We have a history, him and I. The vision of my younger self, nervous and shaking, standing before a general fills my mind. So many years ago, Trap and I were handpicked from hundreds of men. I savored the attention then, and also the realization that the mission would probably be my last.

We stood in unmarked tan shirts and pants with infer-red reflectors sewn onto our shoulder and backs to allow our visibility under night vision goggles. Standing at attention I felt like a Kamikaze pilot preparing for my final journey and like them took with me only what was necessary to finish the task we were given. Two soldiers confiscated my identification card along with my personal effects, but allowed me to keep my lucky watch. Tonight, my hand instinctively reaches for my wrist to feel the comfort of a time piece lost long ago in another battle on another day. Luck seems oddly out of place in this country and I struggle with my mind as it attempts to escape from the present. I need to get out of here, clear my thoughts, focus, be what I am trained to be. My men and I are alive after countless missions because of my preparation.

I realize I am standing completely still. The base moves like an active ant hill around me. Angry at my lack of concentration I make myself move. Maybe a shower or walk, something will shake off the assault of my past. I need time to gather and strengthen my plan. I clutch at the folder and review the contents in my mind, but even as I attempt to gather and formulate, images of the past spread through me. I continue to walk, conditioned to blend in despite my growing terror. Eventually, I find myself sitting at the back of a small café gripping a latte I don't remember ordering, and reliving a mission I hadn't thought about in many years.

A general's voice echoes through my brain from long ago and speaks of how all the men who took part in this most important mission would be remembered forever. My body was frozen in the position of attention, but my eyes wandered around the room. A photo of the general with the President was on the wall directly in front me and I noticed streaks on the furniture where someone had rubbed a rag on the desk top in a weak attempt to dust. The strap of my rifle dug into the skin on my neck and I listened intently to a man speak of us in the past tense. We were already dead.

I wore no body armor because I would be running a very long way. I refused to have my rifle turned against my countrymen and therefore carried a single magazine with only fifteen rounds. I didn't need food and just a little water for this trip, especially if I died that night. I went over the entire operation from start to finish a dozen times in my head and made a mental tally of my packed equipment. My personal belongings were already neatly packed in a crate and ready to be shipped home. The box sat on my bunk, but not for a trip to the states. I had given instructions for my brothers to divide the contents among themselves if I didn't return. I was as ready as I would ever be.

Trap shifted his weight beside me. The General was finished and stood up sharply. Dismissed, Trap and I both saluted and our commander held the door. On our way out he looked me in the eyes and said "Happy Hunting." I nodded and walked past him into the silent hallway. We were like astronauts making our way to the Apollo 12 rocket. Everyone watched us without a word. Dead men walking.

When I entered the planning room Trap was at the table and handed me an old passport photo of the target. There wasn't anything special about him; in fact he looked like every other man in this part of the world. He must be a very valuable trophy to be worth two American lives. I studied his face and visualized my bullet destroying him.

"See you soon," I whispered putting the photo in a clear plastic cover on my forearm.

Trap stood up with a sigh, "I guess I'm ready too." He handed me a satellite phone, but I refused the offered call. Nothing waited for me back home. Trap grabbed the phone and rolled his chair to the farthest corner of the room. He spoke in low pleasant tones, but after his call he sat dazed and staring at the floor. I imagined his thoughts and pictured his wife and children waiting for his return. The room was quiet, as I played the 600 meter shot I was going to make repeatedly in my head. I saw my bullet breaking through the man's windshield and killing him as he went to his temple for worship. My vision was interrupted by a knock on the door. A soldier leaned in and told us the helicopters were on their way. Trap grabbed his gear and with one last deep breath we were off. It was 3:30 AM.

The night was beautiful and cool with stars covering a huge black sky. We walked in silence and heard the choppers in the distance. Our guys were waiting at the landing pad to shake our hands and wish us well. They walked with us toward the three waiting Blackhawks, everyone all smiles and jokes, but as I stepped into our ride and turned to flip them off I saw their expressions had changed. The once smiling faces were now dead.

Even though we were the only ones in the bird, Trap sat right next to me, and we leaned against each other and took a last look at our friends. Then there was only the desert, a wasteland called the cradle of civilization. This was the land I was soon to be released upon. Oddly, I mourned my ex-wife the entire time to our drop off point. I hadn't given her a thought in many months and now pictured myself meeting her for the first time, making love to her, and remembered how her skin felt and tasted. I was very close to her for those moments and regretted everything that had led to our divorce. My whimsical grieving period was short lived, interrupted by the alarm of the helicopter's computer system as we crossed a hostile border into Pakistan.

I watched the ground rush pass like a reel of my entire life. The other birds escorting us were gone and our helicopter banked from side to side as it navigated through trees like driving cones. "One minute," the crew chief yelled. Our ride slowed down and hit the ground just long enough for Trap and me to jump out and sprint into the night. The sound of the chopper quickly faded and was replaced by our breathing as we ran to cover five kilometers of rocky terrain in thirty minutes. We needed to separate from the noise of our entrance quickly and had to be in place for my shot before sunrise or miss the chance to take out our target.

We ran hard, bobbing and weaving through trees and shrubs, determined to make it in position on time. The burning in our lungs didn't stop us from pushing harder. Up small hills and down into river beds we drove ourselves in the shadows of the full moon always pointed west as we traveled deeper into this new country. I knew we were the hottest ticket today and at least forty people were intently watching our progress in the command center.

Washington had to approve a mission such as this so I imagined a room full of spectators getting their thrills in the Pentagon as well.

I started to pull ahead of Trap and purposely fell back out of respect for him, but also began to worry about the mission. I needed prep time for my shot and Trap was panting like a dog. We were barely moving faster than a walk and weren't going to make it before dawn at this pace. I turned off the microphone of my radio and whispered, "I'm going to start to push ahead, and you catch up." He didn't respond, but immediately fell to the ground and grabbed his ankle. I hovered over him confused and tried to examine his leg.

He whispered, "I'll catch up," and was holding his ankle on the ground, but his face was calm and relaxed. Trap was putting on a show for the satellites. His eyes were glowing in the moonlight as he waited for me to say something that would unmask his ruse, but I said nothing. I simply turned and ran towards my target. The general's voice broke the silence of my radio suggesting that we stop the operation. Always the politician, Trap convinced them that the operation should continue. I never slowed and remained silent with my focus on the task. I felt the wind on my face and soon the radio chatter fell silent. All eyes were on me now.

Running along the dark side of a hill I saw the small warming fires and lights of the target's home. Never taking my eyes from the house, I crawled on my belly over the last one hundred feet into a group of bushes at the top of the hill. I pulled out my knife and softly stabbed the earth breaking up the dirt to make a shallow trench. Finally, I climbed in and buried myself. Feeling the pulse of the earth as I lay in my grave, I whispered into my radio, "This is X-ray twenty-seven. I'm home."

There was an immediate response. "Roger twenty-seven, we have eyes on you. You are in good position."

I recognized the voice of the General who sounded on edge and replied softly, "Zero-one, this is X-Ray twenty-seven go ahead with data."

Again the radio blurted a response, "Roger, prepare to copy: wind currently three knots east, barometric pressure..." The general continued to give me all the information I needed to make a deadly and accurate 600 meter shot. For a second I wanted to ask about Trap, but scanned the area and dialed all of the information into the scope of my rifle instead. I checked my details at least five more times and forced my body to be still in order to be invisible in the moonlight.

Waiting for the sun to raise itself, I did what all snipers do and became one with the earth around me. I took deep breaths through my nose to get the smell of this place, heard the wind, and felt the dust rush across my sweat drenched back and neck. The sound of dry leaves as they moved in the breeze whispered to me and each bird spoke intimately as they awakened from their peaceful night. I watched a hornet after a lengthy battle kill a spider and then turned my attention back to the house wondering if I was the hornet or the spider in the battle to come. I opened my eyes close to the blurred ground. The spider lay dead inches from my face and was being torn apart by ants. I was part of this life cycle now and smiled as the sun began to rise.

Four cars were parked in front of the compound and I carefully planned out each shot into them. If I was still alive after, I would wait until the sun was setting directly behind me and then run into it for my escape. I would be almost invisible. The general was still manning the radio when I called in to get an update on changes in the atmosphere. I was excited as I dialed everything into my scope and pulled the cap on my barrel. Lying on my belly covered in dirt I looked over the barrel of my rifle and visualized the perfect shot.

"Twenty-seven, you awake?" the General spoke with concern.

I responded calmly, "Roger, I have activity in the target building."

"We got it over here too. We're reading seven personnel total. It looks like they are heading out. You are a go. You are a go. You are a go!" The general couldn't contain his excitement, but I remained focused.

"Roger, I am a go."

I will not fail became my mantra. The radio was silent while the crowd left the building and began getting into their cars. I removed my front scope cover and glanced at the photo on my arm one last time. I was ready when the gate of the house began to open and dropped my eye in the scope to scan the four cars and truck parked in front of the compound.

The general interjected, "Twenty-seven, this is Zero-one, target normally rides front passenger of tan Mercedes."

"Roger," I called back, but had already spotted my target. He was wearing a white traditional robe and walked out of the house holding a little girl. He was surrounded by fifteen men dressed in Army fatigues and carrying rifles. The target laughed with the child in his arms as his entourage scanned the horizon nervously. I had an overpowering urge to kill him at that very moment, but knew if I was going to have any chance of escape I must wait until all of them were in their cars and unable to detect the direction of my shot.

I kept him in my sights and waited. As his people started to separate and move toward the other cars I watched he and his little girl playfully skipped to their vehicle. He tossed his daughter in the air and I began to sweat. Sweeping across the scene of cars and people my sight crossed a man with binoculars looking toward my position. He stood like a statue focused in my direction. I imagined he heard my pulse as the blood raced through my body and saw my every move. I knew the cost of this mission and fixed my rifle back on the man and child waiting for their smiles to disappear as they were told about my presence. They were almost to their cars. I was sure I'd been spotted and so I waited for my target to be alerted. He was fixed in my sight as he placed his little girl in the backseat of the car. He stood up, stretched his back, watched the activity of his entourage and still nothing happened. He appeared pleased with what he saw and walked to the passenger door.

A breeze blew across and cooled my back. My target and I had become one. He opened his car door and I shifted one last time to ready my shot as a man crossed between us. I almost pulled the trigger thinking he was being warned about me and then watched in amazement as he impatiently waved off his visitor and sat down into the car. I charged my weapon. My target smiled as he shut the door of his car and turned to his little girl in the back seat. I switched my weapon from safe to fire. He was still smiling when his head exploded from the force of the bullet from my 300 WinMag.

As with all tragedy it took only seconds for the crowd below me to realize what had happened. First his driver dove from the car and snatched the little girl from the back seat. I thought he was going to snap her neck as he violently pulled her out and ran into the house. Next, other car doors were opened and heads emerged with expressions of confusion. They began to open fire with their AK-47s wildly in all directions and scatter for cover. I scanned the parking lot to see if anyone had seen the shot. The man with the binoculars was in his car and I watched his expression turn from confusion to anger. He slowly opened the door and once again turned his gaze in my direction. He stood lifting his binoculars to his face and looked straight at me. I pulled the trigger and whispered, "My secret dies with you." The binoculars flew off into oblivion as his body continued to stand with the top of his skull completely gone.

The men around his car jumped out onto the ground. I was too far way to hear them, but I saw their faces and torsos constricting as they screamed in horror. Soon everyone was out of their cars. Some men ran back into the gate of the compound while others kneeled behind the doors of their cars and fired their AK-47's at ghosts. Men barked orders as others peaked like gofers over the door and hood of their cars. I watched their terror as adrenaline and bullets moved in every direction and knew with each one of their panicked breaths the odds of my survival rose. I observed the scene below me turn into comedy as the men ran in circles and dove from car to car in total confusion. I called in, "Zero-one this is Twenty-seven."

The general answered immediately, "Twenty-seven this is Zero-one, go!"

A chill ran down my back as I spoke the words, "Target confirmed."

"Roger," a new voice responded sounding more like an adolescent than a soldier. The game was over as far as the general was concerned. He had relinquished the radio to a boy and it went silent once again. I was alone.

The only task which remained was to survive. I scanned the crowd in front of the house and watched the soldiers on their knees pulling my target out of the car and dragging the body toward the inside gates. As the day continued, the men stopped running and seeking shelter. They probably believed I was gone. I knew I was thrown away on this mission, but at the moment I felt like the most valuable man in the Army and was determined to prove it. I imposed myself upon the frightened crowd with the only means of communication I had at hand. Every time a man got behind the wheel of a vehicle he was shot. I allowed no one to gaze into the distance or venture out of the courtyard of the house. For the rest of the day I made everyone below subscribe to my rules. It only took nine more shots to make them understand my language.

Eventually the sun disappeared behind the horizon and my reign was at an end. I covered the scope on my rifle, dropped the magazine, and pulled out the last two bullets. I buried them in the same hole I had laid in all day. Folding in the butt stock of my rifle, I strapped it on and started to crawl back the way I had come. After cresting the hill I informed command that I was on my way out and wondered if they were surprised. I pictured myself entering the command center, looking all those people in the eyes and smiling at their astonished faces. I felt untouchable as I walked back to the extraction point. I was a man on a leisurely stroll in a park, not someone completely alone in a hostile country. I knew Trap was probably asleep in his own bed by now, and would never recognize his actions as those of a coward. I was without any means to protect myself, but not Trap or my vulnerability seemed important compared to the horror I had caused in the last twenty hours. I thought about how the men had scattered like cockroaches running from a kitchen light and then, laughed out loud. I was the hornet.

"I'm glad someone can find something to laugh about in this heat. Mind if I join you, the other tables are full?" I'm confused for a moment as my mind is jolted into the present, and barely respond to the young woman in fatigues standing before me. I'm not even sure how long I've been sitting in the cafe. Something is very wrong with me.

"I was leaving anyway, the table is yours," I speak hastily, guilty for my lost time.

I grab my folder and reach the door, but hear her call to me, "Sir, you forgot your coffee." I continue running from my ghosts into the fading light without a word.

CHAPTER FIVE

Work has always saved me. Getting lost in the technical aspects and details gives me a semblance of control over the chaos of this war and my part in it. I am calm after my brief disappearance and no one seems to have noticed my absence. I am determined to discipline my thoughts. Back in the TOC, I pick up my mission folder which began yesterday with two pages and now overflows with pictures, maps, and signatures. The simple message **I WAS HERE** is scribbled across the inside of the cover. I recognize the handwriting and know I'll never meet its author. I have followed this message for almost three years. **I WAS HERE** was on a bed frame in Ar Ramadi, on the top of a shower stall in Khost, and found by accident inside a chest of drawers at Bragg.

The stranger's tag is strategically placed so that only a person in my position could discover it, which makes the message more like a whisper than conversation. At one time I even thought it was Mike, but the messages continued long after he became part of the sand in this place. I suppose the repeated signature is proof that the soldier has survived his rotation or maybe it is simply his greeting to me like a wink or nod before I take over the show. On this day his familiar handwriting makes me think of him back home relaxing at a bar or lying next to several beautiful women on a beach somewhere. After twenty hours of continuous stress his statement seems more like gloating and for a moment I hate him. I close the folder so that I don't see the writing anymore and lie to myself that things are exactly how they should be on the first mission of a rotation.

Lighting my cigarette, I take in the room with each inhale. The man next to me huffs at his bad luck at sitting next to a smoker. We both know I'm not supposed to smoke indoors, but at this point no one has bothered to tell me to stop. My neighbor continues hammering away at his keyboard in protest at one of my favorite pastimes. He is holding back his constant urge to yawn and looks exhausted. In fact, everyone in the room looks very tired and despite their five o'clock shadows and un-tucked shirts still hurry about as if they welcome their weariness.

The only common movement I note is an occasional glance at the satellite image of a four building compound on the plasma screen. I had heard the Rangers are on a mission tonight and try to sit back and watch the entertainment in the hope I can forget what is at stake for me and my men later this evening. I need a moment to breathe.

I can see the white heat signatures of people as they sleep in their beds or walk around buildings soon to be destroyed by members of Alpha Company of the 1st Ranger Battalion. Behind the noise of the room, I hear Rangers on their radios as they make their way to their destination. They are less than thirty minutes out from the target and still laugh and talk shit to each other. I almost miss the hyper-structured existence of a private. I imagine the four Chinooks and three Blackhawks hovering just above the rooftops as a hundred warriors slide down their ropes charging the earth. Chills rush over my body as I think of all those twenty *somethings* running head first into the buildings and their destiny. Even though those days for me are long past, I still feel their excitement and wonder why things seem to be complicated now, and like the old song, the thrill has gone. Sitting back and envious, I take little consolation that my team and I are not the only ones on the planet working on Christmas Day.

I return to the piles of paper and maps that have over-taken my desk, and drive all reminiscent memories and noise out of my mind. I need to look at my mission one last time with a fresh eye before presenting it for my team's scrutiny. The superstitious side of me knows that this first mission sets the pace and tone for the rest of the deployment. The boys and I have to be on point tonight, locked up tight and only capable of perfection. Shortly the people in this room and in secret spaces back in the States will be looking at satellite images and hearing my voice through the speakers broadcasting final instructions to my team.

I have one more task to complete before I go. Finding a large black marker I begin blacking out the mission name on the folder. Watching the block letters slowly disappear, I imagine the instant that each member of my team could potentially die and picture their faces as they slip away into nothingness. I see my own death and envision the last thing I recognize is the dark sky seen through the green lens of night vision goggles. Unlike the anticipation of the Rangers moments away from glory, I understand the costs and feel the weight of deep loss. I know it is pointless to review my mission again despite my desire to linger at my desk. It is time to go.

The radios fall silent for the first time since the Rangers started their flight. They must be close. Someone calls out that they are five minutes out and the room is suddenly still. Each man becomes frozen into a large piece of stone as they look up to watch the mission begin. The screen becomes their god, but the only thing on my mind is all the mistakes within my plan. I want to pick up the file and throw it across the room. I want to hunt down the mousy little man who dropped the stuffed folder on my desk in the first place and beat him to a pulp. Pushing myself and my nerves away from the desk, I glance at the screen on the wall and see the helicopters are directly above the objective building. Infer-red lights pulse in a cloud of dust the rotor blades wash up. Everyone is out of their offices. I feel the adrenaline in the room as the once busy men now stand in silence with open mouths. It only took two Rangers sliding down their ropes and hitting the ground to hold everyone in the room in awe.

Reaching over to close my laptop, I work my way out of the room. Behind me the sounds of shooting and screams pour from the radio speakers and the white heat signatures of those who slept in the house are robbed of their peace and start to run in panic. Due to their speed, most of the bodies never have a chance to grab their weapons to retaliate against the young Americans. "Rangers Lead the Way," I whisper to myself and enter the code that allows me to exit the command room. I'm on deck.

It is cold as I walk toward the team house and this time I do not pause or reflect. The clock is ticking and there are only a few hours before we load our choppers. I no longer care about anything except the papers that struggle to fall out of the folder. I make myself walk slower and attempt to conquer the dread engulfing me. No place for doubt or fear here, but they still find their way. Forcing myself to remain calm, I shove my hands deeper into my pockets in an effort to hide from the cold, but there isn't any point. Hiding from the cold is like hiding from death. It will always creep in no matter what precautions you take.

The house is empty, but fast being made into a home. The beginnings of a mural created out of Maxim magazines and FHM girls take over one wall. Everything is clean and re-arranged. A couch was built out of scrap wood, area rugs cover the plywood floor, and a plasma screen is mounted. Every bed is made except for mine. I haven't bothered to sleep or eat in two days. Sitting amidst the photos of women in lingerie and bikinis I take a last peak at my folder and enjoy my first taste of solitude in almost three days. The scribbled **I WAS HERE** catches my attention once again and I pull out my marker to block it out, but instead mark **ME TOO** underneath the anonymous message. This is the first time I intentionally left a trace of my presence in this war. The violation of protocol feels good and for a brief second I enjoy my rebellion. I think I'm smiling and all memories seem safely locked up as my thoughts clearly focus on the mission. I'm fine. It was just a stutter, a momentary weakness.

Too quickly it's time to find my men and begin our deployment. The cold air burns my lungs as I approach a large off-white aluminum dome. In my first deployment the Bagram gym was two dumbbells on a muddy patch of earth. Now the Gym consists of a building the size of a soccer field complete with plasma screens for entertainment and every piece of equipment is top of the line. The gym cost millions and might be seen as frivolous by some when compared with the regular Army's lack of body armor, but I know it is important. It feeds the vanity of these men and it is their vanity that keeps them motivated.

The smell of the room is the first thing I notice. It's thirty-five degrees outside, but the young Rangers who are at the bench closest to the door in their black short-shorts don't seem to care. They lift weights as if they are in a heated competition with every other man in the room. I know most feel like they are the junior varsity of the world, but the truth is Ranger platoons are the most lethal fighting units on the planet. Next to them at a pull-up bar is a group of SEALs with their NAVY sweat shirts broadcasting their affiliation. Everyone hates to work with them because they're the most arrogant and passing a SEAL on his twentieth pull-up I can't stop myself. With a grin I announce "You know God created Rangers so that SEALs could have heroes. No, no don't stop on my account. Glad to see you're good at something." I keep walking and feel all of their eyes fixed on my back. The only people in the room I might welcome as additions to my unit are the FBI hostage rescue team. Even though they are basically cops, I enjoy their intellect and conversation. They're gathered together in the far corner of the dome in their matching sweat suits and huge handlebar mustaches. They are the only ones in the gym dressed for the cold weather.

In the middle of the room, among the clank of weights and straining grunts, I find my men. They look more like a shabby garage band standing around a bus stop than a team of highly trained and skilled soldiers. Some of them wear sweaters with flip-flops, and others, band t-shirts with camouflage pants. Marti has a bright red Santa hat on top of his head. The only things that match among them are their sleeves of tattoos and their resemblance to beggars on the street. They are relaxed and content and I can hear their bellows of laughter over the noisy gym. None of them know the feelings of regret and sorrow that have suddenly begun to consume me or the dead who cling to my thoughts. Tormented, I continue across the gym to take them from their peace and into the world for which they were built.

Q's face reflects the wear of too many days running around the desert with me. He commands attention and respect from the team despite his mental instability. Everyone is focused upon him as he talks. He scans the gym as he speaks with a squinting smile and stops when he sees me. He looks as if he's seen a ghost. The rest of the team turns and their smiles vanish as well. Marti removes his Santa hat and they huddle together, frozen, focused upon me, resembling some sort of distorted nativity scene. There is no need to speak. I motion my head towards the door and the team follows me toward the exit.

All of the men in the room understand what I am doing and can imagine what lies ahead for us. The SEALs stop and watch me cross to the exit as the oldest of them nods. I return the greeting and continue toward the door. We had met five years ago on top of Tukar Ghar and as he falls from my field of view, I wonder if he remembers me and that horrible day. The earth is so small and combat is our bond and why we will be brothers forever. I can see every friend I have in the world in the reflections on the wall as I pass. Each of these men holds a piece of my being and among them my life exists. I have no family or friends back home to claim, all have fallen away over the years. War takes that from you. The young Rangers pause their workout to watch us leave. I flash them a nod and smile. They look like little boys, fresh and without scars. Their innocence catches me off guard and I find myself entranced by their young pale faces. They are the opposite of my men who have been to battle and carry with them the weight and wounds of their experience. I allow myself a moment to enjoy the sight and then I'm out the door.

The only sounds are our footsteps on the gravel path. Holding the door of the team house open for my men, I try to envision each man at every point of the mission as they pass me, but they rush by too fast. I can't keep up. Pausing outside I hungrily gasp one last deep breath of cold air and look at the night sky. I can't stop the momentum and feel their eyes lock on me as I enter. My men are gathered around the table waiting expressionless for me to brief them. Focus. There is no more time for confusion, ghosts, or doubt. I am surrounded by friends, but it is their faith in me that fills my chest with anxiety. None of us can hesitate. I smile as I step to the head of the table. "Listen up," I announce in my most commanding voice and start the brief. It's my show and the only thing that I feel certain about is that people are going to die tonight.

CHAPTER SIX

I am startled from my nightmare by its horror. Even though the sound of the helicopter is comforting, catching a few moments of dreamless sleep proves to be impossible. These new nightly visitors are developing more consistency. I look around me and most of the boys are dozing, catching rest while they can. Their faces are relaxed as if they are children, seamless in innocence and without fear. I know the wait will soon be over, but Marti's expression of terror from my dream still holds and his screams echo in my brain. I sit sweating despite the frozen air rushing into the bird. The fear is real. The ravaging dreams are only reliving memories.

The radios come alive just before dawn with intelligence updates and my nightmares recede only to be replaced by another. We are five minutes out from the objective. There are more fighters at the target building than originally reported and evidence surfacing of two machine gun nests preparing for our arrival. Everything has the makings of an ambush. After hearing what is waiting for us, the crew chief looks to me and simply asks, "Are we still a go?" I don't bother to answer him, but lift my rifle and pull the charging handle, letting it slip out of my fingers. The weapon jolts to life loading a bullet into the barrel and is ready to fire. My men also hear the *Intel* as they awake. They remain un-phased as they ready their weapons, saving themselves one step before hitting the ground. We knew what we were getting into and agreed to the terms before ever leaving base for this mission. No words need to be spoken.

The throttle opens up and the choppers flare to a complete stop a hundred feet above the ground. I fight the g-force trying to pull me to the floor. The ropes fall and our slide into combat is textbook. On the ground the darkness envelopes us and my men and I find ourselves hopelessly outnumbered and pinned down. We are suddenly in the fight for the first time during this deployment.

Sweat pours down my face, blood rushes through my body, and I am terrified. I look to my right and see Doc hovering over one of my boys. His frantic routine slows. I don't need any more information to know that Pete is gone. Doc instinctively turns in my direction and shakes his head "no". I watch him drag the body closer to an alley and out of the way of the battle. I understand that I am responsible for this soldier's death, but my self-loathing will have to wait.

The sound of choppers overtakes the gunfire. They are covering us from the sky in a racetrack formation. Right above me a Chinook helicopter making a gun run is banking so hard that the door gunner's body is almost horizontal to the ground as the chopper turns to avoid small arms fire. Our transport leaves behind a falling trail of brass and spent casings pouring out of the two machine guns. Another helicopter roars overhead and this time it is so low that it shatters the glass of the second and third story windows of buildings that line the street. The gunners unleash their 20mm canons and the buzz sound causes every enemy fighter to duck for cover, giving us a slight reprieve from the bullets solely directed at us. These pilots and their crews live by a simple motto: "Night Stalkers don't quit". Today as they keep us alive on the ground, they are putting those words to the test.

The target building is 100 meters to my front. The distance can be covered in about fifteen seconds by my men, but under this gunfire those short seconds would be suicide. Instead, I instruct them to focus on the rooftops and the RPK automatic weapons that have spun into the fight. My boys are in pairs, most of them kneel down behind cover with their backs against each other; one faces the target building, while the other scans the rooftops looking for opportunities to present themselves. They look focused and are settling into their environment. I'll give them a few more minutes before the call for assault.

The gunfire from the rooftops suddenly stops. I look to Q and the confusion on his face confirms the silence. Marti seems lost as he scans the ledges in every direction. A sharp sting of terror suddenly fills my mind. Something is coming. Soldiers are all the same whether they are from America or Afghanistan. We share the same DNA no matter on what side we fight, and just as my men would slow to catch a peek at a car wreck, our enemy on this day does the same.

The battle pauses, muscles tighten in preparation for the inevitable impact and my fear swells.

"Lock it up men, fresh magazines," I sternly call over the radio. The action takes half a second and for these soldiers requires no more thought than swatting a fly and allows their eyes to continue scouring the surroundings. The massive iron-gate standing guard over the target building creaks in movement and the air fills with the sound of locking weapons as my men turn ready. The gothic ornamentation begins to fall under shadow as the gate swings inward. The screech of metal on metal ends and the gate fully open reveals a dark world within. Squinting, I try to see, but my eyes fail me. I hear movement coming from the shadows behind the Great Wall that surrounds the objective, but without visuals I am guessing. The noise builds and a car motor roars to life followed by the battle cries of countless men from the darkness.

"203, now and keep it coming!" I yell to my grenadiers. Almost immediately my need is answered by the metallic thump of grenade launchers. Into the emptiness behind the gate they land and light the cavern with flashbulb intensity. The battle cries die and are replaced by panicked shrieks of pain. "Hit them again," I respond without emotion.

More comforting thumps follow, but this time there are no screams of panic, just the growing thunderous call for battle from within their keep. I fight the fear in my voice and launch a warning, "Get ready boys, here they come."

Eye deep in my scope, finger sliding into my trigger, one last breath, maybe one of my last, and it begins. Into the sun a truck bolts out of the darkness heading right at us. Two men stand in the bed of the truck. The rocket propelled grenades they hold fire simultaneously. One screams over my head while the other finds its way to a car and explodes. Two of my men hiding behind the vehicle fall away onto their backs trying to escape the inferno. Nova moves just in time, but Olson is engulfed in flames, his hands clawing at burning eyes. He rolls and flails wildly as Nova dives onto his friend trying to smother the blaze. The last thing I see before turning back to the battle is Nova fighting to remove Olson's helmet. I attempt to block out the man's screams, but his pain cuts through the gunfire to the deepest part of me.

The truck that initiated their charge rams clumsily into a parked car and the force throws the men out of the bed, skipping them off the asphalt. One smashes his head into the curb, dead on impact, while the other tries to get back into the target building. He runs for his life limping as fast as he can. His head jerks forward from the force of one of our shots and his body slams onto the street. Following the truck are forty men running and screaming to Allah. Each one of them is opening up their AK-47s on full auto. Bullets skip and snap in every direction. Their eyes are filled with fire and hate and they are bearing down on me and mine.

I shoot two, who fall in shock, disbelieving even as they die. My boys take care of most of the rest. One of the enemy's AK-47 is empty from the initial assault and he charges Q, who still has plenty of ammunition in his weapon, but slings his own rifle behind his back and lunges toward the enemy. Q tackles him in mid-stride and bashes his head in with a piece of nearby stone. Without pause or hesitation, he then returns to his position and sector of fire. A lone enemy survivor sensing his isolation turns to retreat. One step is all we allow before his entrails are torn from his body by our bullets. I am on my feet moving closer to the target building as the lull in the battle begins. Finding a home behind a pile of stones, I call my men to shift forward and rest for a moment surveying the damage. Q and his boys move along the building to my right and creep up to my position while Marti and the rest of the team find a spot across the street. Sliding on his side over to me, Q digs into one of his pouches. "I'll get charges ready."

"Patience, I don't think that is all they have in store for us. If need be, we wait till dark." My words mean a full day of battle as the enemy attempts to pick us apart, but Q doesn't even blink as he processes the order, nods, and backs into his position. Using a pile of rubble to support his weight, Nova pulls guard holding his weapon with one hand while cradling the other in his armpit. I acknowledge his presence still in the fight. He can only shake his head low and fail at any attempt to mask his pain. I notice the burns that cover his torso and can only imagine what his hand must look like, but now is not the time to probe. The moment is stolen by rustling behind the gate. I am closer to my goal and see soft silhouettes moving within the dark. Raising my weapon I pull the trigger. A shadow falls and a woman shrieks and cries. From behind the wall the voice of a man yells and barks orders. I can't make out the *Pashto*, but his demands are met with more sobs and finally stillness.

My next impulse is to take advantage of our new proximity and order a round of grenades to be thrown into the building, but a ghost appears at the gate as the sun rises through the clouds and stops us all in our tracks. Flowing white robes caught in the breeze and early morning rays give an illusion of those before us as floating. First one appears and then another and another, one by one stepping into the light, all of them with heads bowed in a forced reverence. With arms at their sides, the waves of fabric reveal inked hands and fine jewelry. The women move into the street and never look in our direction. Their eyes are lowered and their movement silent. We are all frozen in confusion at this eerily out of place sight. Half of us stay weapons fixed on the target building and the others focus on the seven women that now fan into the street. I flood myself with possible answers to this riddle, but none make any sense. I force patience and watch closely.

The first woman is well into the street and within 30 meters of us when she stops at the body of the man who led the charge. No longer able to contain her emotions and free from the reach of the discipline inside the gate, she wails her pain. In the middle of the battlefield strewn with bodies the women stand among us and weep. My chest tightens with the urge to go and comfort, but they would never allow it. Their culture would stone them to death if I even touched them, so I sit and participate in their suffering as a voyeur. The lead ghost takes a long resigned breath and reveals to me her purpose in this fight even as her tears continue to fall. She kneels down, grabs the AK-47 off the body of the dead, and retreats back towards the building. The other women do the same and their timid steps with heads low prepare themselves for our expected reaction. I am the first to draw and fire upon the woman closest to the gate. My men fall into line mirroring my precedent. In this hell there is always more to give and the war always has more to take.

Our eyes freeze on the stained motionless forms that lay before us, but movement from behind the gate snaps our rifles back to find a new target. A young boy moves without reason into the street. His eyes are swollen with tears. He is drawn by some unseen force and finds his way to a woman, her fine sari now soaked in crimson. The child's sobs ring through the empty streets and he looks into the darkness behind the gate. As the boy kneels beside the dead I take aim. "NO!" Marti yells from across the street. Turning to his voice, I watch him move from cover, running full speed toward the boy. I want to scream go back, find safety, but instead do nothing except wait for him to be taken from me. I turn my weapon back to the boy whose hands are almost to the body and its possession. Everything moves slowly. Shots ring out from behind the gate and my men return fire. Q stands straight up and jumps a pile of bricks running at Marti and screaming for him to get back. The boy grabs the weapon and I pull my trigger taking the child out as the gun fire continues around me.

I see out of the corner of my eye that Q is struggling to get Marti to his feet, but when Marti realizes the boy is gone, he gives up the battle and allows Q to drag him back to us. Two men appear to be doing most of the shooting from the target building and as soon as they are killed the gun fire dies with them. I lean against the rubble and take in the sight of Marti. He is sobbing and completely broken down as he accuses me. "You didn't have to kill him man, he is just a kid! He didn't know what he's doing."

"Shut the fuck up, you almost got us both killed," Q interrupts, slamming his fist into his buddy's gut in hope that sucking for air will silence him. The punch does just the opposite. Marti springs to life pouncing onto Q's shoulders and delivering a swift elbow to his cheek bone. Q isn't fazed by the strike and exhibits perfect Brazilian *Ju Jitsu* form taking his opponent to his back, but this time holds a knife to his throat. Marti knows if Q had any desire to kill him, he wouldn't think twice about the action or repercussions.

My friend lies on his back with eyes wide in fear and yet refuses to be quiet. "You'd like to kill me wouldn't you? So I wouldn't be around anymore to remind you how fucking crazy you are." Q edges the knife with pressure into Marti's throat, but the fallen has lost his fight and crushes his eyes closed as if trying to wake from a terrible nightmare.

"Q," I call to him. Q's body relaxes slightly while lowering the knife a millimeter. "Get back in line." The soldier reacts to his order, snaps to his feet, and in a low run returns to his original position. The knife has disappeared as he draws his weapon and scans the wall in a horizontal motion. Marti stays on his back exhausted from the horror.

"This isn't right, Joe. It shouldn't have to be like this. It never used to be like this." I hear my friend's pain and wonder why I don't share the same sympathy for the child. I look over at the fallen boy and study his body closely. Tiny hands are still clutching the rifle and an expression of pain is frozen forever on his face. I understand why Marti protested, but inside of me nothing stirs. I look deep, but find only emptiness. Marti's eyes are still trickling tears and I can see his agony. He is right. There was a time when this type of killing would not have been an option, but that time is long past and only a faint memory on this day.

"Olson is not doing so good," Doc's voice brings my radio to life. "If he doesn't get out of here soon he won't make it." I want to tell him I will call in the choppers to take the soldier to base. I want to move all my men back to safety, but those thoughts quickly fade as the gravitational pull of the mission takes its hold. There is more work to be done. The sun is rising and burns away the chill of evening. As soon as night falls once again, I will take my objective and complete my assignment, but until then I'm forced to ponder the truth of our first battle. No ground was gained or lost. As time passes no history will be written about this struggle at dawn or the warriors who sacrificed themselves for this war. There is a cost and the cost is too high.

CHAPTER SEVEN

After hours of battle the sun is finally gone, and we are bone weary as the stars are masked by ominous thunderheads rolling over head. We get a call that the angels over our heads are pulling out due to the inclement weather heading our way. "You gave' em hell today," the crew chief from my helicopter broadcasts to all of us on the ground. In unison my boys howl upward to the sky in answer to the crews above. They can't hear us, but always look back as they fly away home.

"I'll see you tomorrow," I radio and turn to the target building.

Hearing the helicopters fade into the distance my attention focuses ahead and into the coming night. I've had my route planned into the building for hours, but it won't be passed to my men until full darkness can cover our advance. My urge is to call for the assault, but I know patience is needed. My enemy has hit us with their best. Wave after wave sent after us from inside the building. All of it handled and neutralized. At first their battle cry could be heard for miles, but as the day wore on, it was our guns and aim that reduced their warrior spirit. Their last charge was nothing more than a column of specters appearing from the gate with weapons in hand and heads slouched already accepting their fate. The more that came the more we slaughtered until they finally stopped.

My boss and the brass watched us on screens back at base and those who had interest back in Virginia praise our success from the comfort of their arm chairs. They only count the bodies they see from the drones that circle overhead. No one bothers to ask the name of the man I lost, nor do they care about the condition of Olson. Their giddy schoolgirl excitement spilling from the radios does not match the sight I see on the ground. Never mind the mounds of men, women, and child that lie between us and the objective. Never mind that Olson is so badly burned that his browned teeth now protrude from where his lips once hung. He clings to life by a thread, anchored by Doc's vigilant care and settled by almost lethal doses of morphine. It was too dangerous to lift him out under fire and too late for a change in plans.

The sun fades and the temperature starts to drop below freezing. Time slows as the wind and shadows strengthen. Patience. I wait and the adrenaline stops its flow. Every man on my team gives up their cold weather gear so that Doc can swaddle Olson like a baby, but still he shivers violently. It's a miracle he lived through the day and if he survives through the night, he still faces a long battle with infection before him. One way or another I promise to get him home.

I search the faces of my men. They are exhausted, but focused and running on their chemical stream of amphetamines. They will follow without question. Marti avoids my eyes, Q ever watches, and the silence envelopes me like a living thing. I sit against the chilling stones and close my eyes for a moment as those around me remain vigilant. The images behind my lids erupt and claw for attention. Patience. Mike's smiling face passes through my mind's eye. Mike must have beaten his demons; but mine remain, even now pushing their way to the surface.

My mind steals away from the cold and the horror of this night as the past once buried so deep overtakes the present. The images erupt violently in the blaze of a North African sun in August and I escape from the numbing cold of this place. Even as I hear the distant thunder of the Afghanistan night, I am consumed by the memories of an ancient sun on another continent and cannot shake its grasp.

The African helicopter crew looked at me as if I was insane, and perhaps I was when I jumped out of their bird and ran off into the steaming night. I was a rookie going out into the fray alone and my training wheels were off. The months of total devotion to my craft and work were starting to pay off; I was on my way to kill a man in service of America. I ran toward an unnamed village through the cover of darkness and felt alive with the rush of fear. I crept along the outskirts of small settlements and nomadic camps, passing through their land and tribal grounds like a thief in the night. After almost an hour of running I found a home and began my watch on a hill with the village below.

I remember lying in my own piss and shit baking on the African hill for two hellish days waiting to hear a sound from my radio. I watched from my shallow grave completely alone with nothing but my thoughts, a pack of amphetamines, and 300 WinMag sniper rifle. The stillness and repetition brought me to and from madness twice. My boss was testing me.

I monitored the inhabitants as they washed themselves, cooked their meals, and when they switched out their guard shifts, or argued who was off sides as they played soccer. I got to know them and informed my boss. Only protected by a thin layer of dirt I threw on myself, sun-block, and my rifle, I reported with methodical precision every hour.

"23 men, 4 roaming guards, 2 goats"

"23 men, 6 roaming, 2 goats"

"21 men, 2 roaming, 1 goat, they ate the other goat for dinner."

By the end of the second day a convoy of trucks rolled in before sunset. I called the event into the team. My boss quickly replaced the sleepy voice on the other end and wanted me to confirm the target's arrival. I scanned the group below as they hugged and greeted each other. My boss grew more and more agitated the longer I couldn't answer. My heart started to pound making it difficult to hold my rifle steady. The smiles and embraces below quickly stopped and they grouped together in silence looking toward the last vehicle. Time stood still.

The two days I spent visualizing this moment and driving myself mad were not wasted. The training dictated that I start with the leadership and it only took about half a second to find out who was in charge. I saw a man standing tall and looking completely disgusted by what he viewed around him. I pulled back my sleeve to see the picture taped to my arm and confirmed the target. Scanning his face I noticed he was the only one wearing jewelry. I found my target.

"I have confirmation of the target arrival," I called on the radio.

"Go ahead," my boss answered swiftly.

"Eighteen pax arrived along with the target making four-zero men in area of operation," I reported.

"Hold tight, we will be there in one hour," my boss panted back. For the first time in hours I shifted around in my hole trying to wake my lower back and legs which had been asleep for a day. The tingling pricks of blood starting to flow in my extremities painfully swelled through my body. "Cevera, you awake?" my boss' voice was a welcomed sound.

"No," I responded and knew it wouldn't be long now. I tried my best to pop my neck and replace my finger on the trigger well.

"We are 4 kilometers out."

"Thank fucking god, did you bring me something to eat? I'm fucking starving"

"See you in ten minutes." Those were the sweetest words I'd ever heard. The thought of waiting ten more minutes almost brought me to tears.

Looking at people through a scope was like seeing characters on television; the scope was a completely dehumanizing filter. They were no longer people about to die, and in my case they were nothing more than obstacles to my comfort. I scanned my target, who was now sitting alone at the head of a table. I surveyed the current wind conditions and adjusted my sight accordingly. The men below turned to face the direction of a sound and although I could not hear anything below, I knew the operation was about to start. The entire village prepared for their noisy intruder and I found my man. He was jogging up and down his defense line barking orders to his men. All were focused on the hilly horizon when a set of head lights appeared. They shifted into place readying their weapons and themselves for combat.

"We're here," my boss announced, "we go on your mark."

I switched my rifle to fire, took a deep breath and acquired my target in the scope. He knelt behind a line of men pointing at the truck moving toward them. They were all dead and didn't know it. I was about to unleash America's vengeance on the group below for tampering with local diamond production and killing a village of recent Catholic converts and its missionaries. The sun started to set and the sky grew hungry and agitated completely defusing the lights of the truck coming toward them, but I saw their fear. The first round was away and the body of my target flew forward from the force of my bullet completely knocking over the men he hid behind.

The men below fell into confusion and responded with a hail of bullets focused on the truck rolling down the hill. They shouted and screamed as they emptied their weapons at nothing. The rebels gathered around their only dead man and wept like babies, while others reloaded their weapons and continued to shoot at the empty truck which sputtered out and died. Chaos and panic had completely taken hold of the village below. I found number two running behind the ranks yelling at his men and pointing at the truck. He was still giving orders when the bullet spun him around and knocked the life out of him. His men scattered. They were becoming the walking dead as they dove for cover.

Slowly squeezing the trigger I searched for anyone that might want to take charge of the situation or discover my location. Watching the turmoil below reminded me of my boss' favorite saying, "Everything is a weapon". If those below had bothered to take their attention off the truck, they would have noticed a line of men walking toward their rear ready to open fire, or detected the position of a deadly sniper. *Everything is a weapon.*

I shifted my weight and barrel to cover my team as they made their way into the village and continued to call out the numbers and positions of the enemy. There was a slight delay between the muzzle flashes of the rifles and the sound getting to me. My heart pounded with excitement and I forgot about my stench and pain for the moment. I dropped another man as he looked in the direction of my team. I was their guardian angel. Two more down and I pulled my eye out of the scope. The team with cold precision walked into the village and killed everything. As the Africans ran into the hills it became a turkey shoot, but I kept my sight in the village and looked for other opportunities. Less than ten minutes later the shooting was over. My team entered huts, rummaged through their belongings, and then set everything on fire. Only the world within my gun sight existed. My thoughts were concentrated on food and a shower when I heard the heavy footsteps and panting. I was so completely focused on the village below I made their same fatal mistake.

Blood charged through my body and panic set in as if a loaded gun was pointed to my head. I reacted in the way all snipers do and played possum. A good sniper is a coward. I lay there, prayed with my head in the dirt, and hoped I was still buried enough to be missed. The gasps came closer until I was sure he would be on top of me at any moment. With my face in the ground I could not see him. The sounds of his heavy panting were now my eyes. His breath was closer. I struggled to reach my knife as he collapsed on the ground, sobbing. I was no more than four feet from him as he pounded the ground. He was weeping and yelling in his native tongue. This man was a giant shaking the earth with his fists and far too close for me to use my rifle. I wasn't sure if it was cocked or even had any bullets left. I wiggled my toes trying to get some blood flow to my legs and attempted to keep myself from shaking. I couldn't reach the blade and terror washed over me. He was on his feet again and walking towards my trench. The back of my head faced him, but I could feel the earth pulse through my cheek from his steps as he neared. I closed my eyes and then he stopped.

Was he holding his breath? I was sure that he had seen me, and forced myself to move. I rose to my knees and charged him like a NFL lineman. We fell to the ground with me on top and I grabbed for his neck hoping to end this quickly. He was too strong and pulled my right hand away. I was off the ground as he worked to stand up, but managed to wrap and lock my legs around him. The giant placed both his fists on my chest and shoved me off like a rag doll. A sharp pain in my ankle ripped through me as he broke my hold and the air was pushed from my lungs.

He began to circle me like a professional wrestler. I assumed my best boxing stance and prepared for his next attack. His left foot dug into the ground and he charged forward. I saw stars as his shoulder drove into my ribs and I was airborne, but I had wrapped my legs around him again and forced us into the rocky ground. This time he was on top and hammered into my sides with his fists. Each shot felt like a baseball bat smashing into my body and with each blow I found it harder to protect myself. I was about to lose the fight and imagined my death at his hands. He sensed my submission and his pounding began to slow. The African looked down at my face to see my condition. As we made eye contact, I realized his mistake.

His hands had fallen to my chest to rest. Sitting up quickly, I drove my left thumb through his right eye. He screamed and tried to back away, but my legs were tight around him in an attempt to close the distance between me and his blows. I refused to let him go again. He screamed straight into my ear and fell hard on top of me, clawing at the hole in his face where his eye once lived. I leaned in and grabbed hold of his collar and pulled him as close as a lover. Struggling to breath under his weight I felt my face grow wet with his sweat and blood. My ear rang painfully from his scream. At that moment my boss called on the radio advising me to come down to the village. Hearing his voice was a reminder. I was on my own and there would be no one coming to save me.

My enemy tried to rise, but I pulled the collar tighter and strangled his breathing. I yanked hard with my last bit of strength until my hands and fore-arms were on fire from the strain. He struggled to wrench away from me by jerking his entire body, but unlike him I was committed. I would not hesitate. I was a killer. We were the only two beings on the planet.

I don't know how much time passed as I looked up at the sky and felt his life recede. With my left arm still pinned under him, I cherished each deep breath I took and allowed exhaustion to take me. My boss crackled over the radio, "You coming down or what?" Without a response, he continued, "You did a great job today boy."

I limped my way down the hill and fought against the dull pain in my ribs and ankle, but would tell no one of my battle. I didn't want anyone to know I made such a rookie mistake, an error that could have endangered the team. I was willing to die for their approval and didn't want them to doubt me.

I stifle my hysterical laugh at my own need for acceptance as the memories fade and the icy rain begins to fall. Suddenly, I am back in this cold place of waiting. The memories of the dead African's frozen eyes and open mouth cling to me and I am drenched in sweat despite the cold. The storm is coming with full force outside the wall and rattles the ancient gate announcing its presence with deep crashes of lightning. The dead surrounding me are illuminated with each electric flash and for a moment I'm sure I have lost my mind, trapped between what was and is. I raise my face to the freezing rain and let the cold shock me awake. The radio comes to life and I press my fist into the freezing stone until the pain makes me stop. I will not stumble, not now. I grab hold and instruct my men to stay out of sight and to remain completely silent. I know my enemy within the walls wonders if we are still here.

The guards who peek over the barrier to look for us will soon stop, because they won't be able to stand this cold. Their hands will voluntarily put down their weapons in favor of starting a fire to warm themselves. Being soaked to the bone will cause their discipline to lapse. They will relax, gather around the fire to eat, and their social culture will allow their minds to embrace the conversation rather than the threat lurking just outside. That is when I will strike. When I smell food, hear laughter, and as they try to forget the people they lost today, I will walk into this building and bring death with me.

CHAPTER EIGHT

My men and I are in the same set of circumstances as our enemy, each movement brings the
shock of a frozen uniform coming in contact with a
wet body. My hands are numb and toes frozen. I
work to control the chattering of my teeth and hear
the quiver in the voices of my men at each update as
they get into position for our assault. Moving closer
to the target building I stay in the shadows. All my
men, despite the boisterous life we lead, are trained
to be invisible. I don't worry about the focus or discipline of these soldiers. I think back to those long
nights in Ranger School, a task that all my men endured. We are cut from the same cloth and have the
ability to turn adversity into an ally. The storm
spikes.

Sheets of sleet and freezing rain pour down upon us. Q and I have our back to the front wall of the
target building. Q with his eye in his scope scans the
wall above. His infer-red laser makes a sweeping

motion along the top of the walls and into any possible window that could pose a threat. We are buried deep into each other with my shoulder in his diaphragm and his weapon resting on top of my helmet. I take a moment to survey the street we just crossed, but any shift in Q's demeanor is more than an alert that something is wrong. The street to my front looks completely abandoned. The lifeless bodies strewn about become masked as the rain drops defuse their lines making them seem part of the landscape. The charred remains of the truck look at home, but poorly parked under the dim stormy sky.

This is what my enemy sees, but it is not reality. The resting battlefield is an illusion, a slight of hand afforded to us by years of training and focus. A flashbulb of lightning strikes close to the west. The ground pulses from the power of the energy absorbed and I feel it through my soaked boots. It's the kind of strike that would terrify me as a kid and now gives power and strength. The thunder follows and for a millisecond the storm reveals my men huddled together deep within the dark crevices of night. All of them are watching me with their weapons locked into a firing position. I wave them forward as the lightning strikes again and then they quickly vanish into the darkness.

Tilting my head outward I get a slight view inside the gate. Their fires are lit and it is almost time. The strobe effect of the storm catches my men moving forward. I blink the rain out of my eyes, look across the gate, and see Marti staring straight back at me with all the boys in tow. Holding my hand out extending one finger, I signal to my men one minute. Marti drops his head into the sight of his weapon and the men do the same. The boss back at base calls in to me with the approving "we are looking good." Armed with the blessings of the powers that be and the smell of sweet aromatic tea in the air, I reach into my pocket and pull a flash bang grenade. Marti does the same and simultaneously we pull the pins and toss them inside. Whatever lies on the other side of this wall or whatever weapon points in my direction does not matter. I know I've increased the odds of my men surviving the next ten steps they take, but fear of the possible outcome of the next thirty seconds overwhelms me. God, let me be strong.

At the gate we turn inside to the building. I can feel Q's weapon hovering over my shoulder ready to extend his will and Marti is my reflection as we move in. The bang of the concussion grenades send a wave of fireworks and panic. My first few steps find a man holding a tea cup. He is frozen in time, his face a cartoon of shock when the tea cup shatters. Betrayal screams from his eyes as the next bullet hits him square in the chest. Ten feet into the objective three more find their end. Marti and my men swarm the front court yard. We are on line almost shoulder to shoulder advancing to the house. I look to Marti and nod. "See you on the other side," I tell him as he takes the boys toward the front door.

Q and I break to the left heading down a small walk way and work our way to the back door trying to prevent any attempt of escape. I want these people alive if at all possible. Death for my target and his henchmen would be too easy. They need to suffer, endure, and most of all, pay. We make our last turn to the back door and find two men standing guard with their backs to us. They are listening to the gun fight raging in the front of the house as we move in for the kill. Slinging my weapon I move closer. On my last step, he senses my presence and turns to face me, but it is too late. He tries to grab his gun, but I cut the strap. My blade makes a sweeping slash across his chest and his weapon falls to the ground. My arm is already around him as he attempts to run and my elbow crushes the back of his head into my collar bone. His mouth opens to scream, but no sound escapes as my arms close around his throat. The rear naked choke is both efficient and effective. I leave just enough space for his last image to be of me and his world filled with terror. I let him fall away, never looking down. Q is wiping his knife clean on the other guard who lies in a pool of blood. Q steps to me, places his hand on my right shoulder and rests his barrel on top. We move in.

I crack open the side door and see an empty staircase leading to the second floor. Fixing my barrel to the top of the stair I step in followed by Q with his back locked into mine and his barrel fixed on the way we came. Together we stop before we reach the top and Q turns to face the front. We move onto the second floor into a long hallway with two doors at the end and another staircase leading to the front door. A man flies up the front stairs barking orders and pointing his finger at the invaders below, but freezes when he sees us. Q's shot to the head sends him flying off the landing and disappearing out of sight in a crash of broken bones. I reach up to punch through the only light bulb in the hallway. Darkness falls as the hot glass of the bulb shatters and brings a sense of warmth to my frozen body. I take a deep breath and step closer to the doors of my objective.

"First floor is clear," Marti calls.

I whisper back, "We are on the second, kill the power to the house, and get the staircase at the front door on lock down."

"Roger, power off in 30 seconds," he answers me obviously on the move.

The house goes black within seconds and the door to my right blasts open as five armed men rush out. Q and I mow them down, leaving the enemy as a pile in front of the opening. One more room left. My target and his sons must be inside. I slide up to the door, crank up my headset and lean over so that it makes contact with the wall. I hear whispering and light footsteps pacing directly on the other side. The footsteps grow louder and the door latch begins to rise. Q hears it too and prepares for the worst. We step back, deeper into the hallway and further from the ambient light creeping through the few windows.

The door opens. Under the green hue of my night vision goggles I see a figure softly slip into the hallway carrying an AK-47 slung low at his waist. He steps forward to peak down the staircase at the activity below and starts backpedalling toward Q and me. Next out of the room is an old man. His limp gives him away as the one I am looking for and he's followed by two young men in their early twenties, his sons.

The man with the AK steps back towards us, allowing room for the old man to make his way fully into the hallway. The target freezes so abruptly that his son walks into him while struggling to get a foot hold in the dark. I don't shoot the guard in fear that my bullet will go clean through him and kill my objective or one of his sons. Stepping to the side signals Q to take over. Knowing a close kill with his M-4 is not an option, he draws a full magazine from his vest and raises his hand over his head. Holding the magazine like a dagger he keeps his weapon steady on the target just in case. By the time the enemy realizes we are there the old man is cringing to avoid the inevitable. Q extends himself bearing down on the man, who doesn't even see the beast that takes his life. His body thuds heavily to the floor with the entire front portion of his head caved in. His forehead oozes brain matter glistening brilliantly in the low light. The old man has no time to mourn his loss and I doubt if he cares. He finds my weapon in his face as Q and I push him and his sons back into the room checking for more hostiles and booby traps all the way. We find the rest of the family huddled in the corner.

I call in we have our target and request choppers to get us out of here. My boss sends excited congrats and clapping can be heard in the background. I guess they enjoyed the show. I don't respond with thanks or acknowledge their praise, but quickly get on my radio and send a detail to retrieve Olson and Pete's body. We leave the old man and his family bound, blindfolded, and gagged in the upstairs room with a couple of my guys to watch over them. I need to see to my men and hurriedly step over countless bodies trying to avoid the blood and debris of death. I reach Doc as he gives instructions to his detail to place Pete's body in the bag. What is left of Pete's face is swollen and grey from the exposure to the rain. He is dead less than twelve hours and is unrecognizable. I think of his wife having to see him this way and turn back to the living. Olson is still wrapped tight in our jackets and shakes violently. "I can't give any more morphine; his heart rate is starting to slow. I don't know how he isn't screaming from the pain," Doc tells me.

I kneel next to Olson losing my words when I see the agony in his eyes. I tell him how brave he is and that it's almost over. I tell him he will be home soon and how proud I am of him and that he is a great soldier. He looks at me with his remaining eye as I speak, but I don't know if he can hear or see me. His left ear is completely burned away. He struggles to respond until his eyes roll back into his head and he passes out. I can't leave him yet as the empty words of so many rush into my mind. . ."you did good, boy". . ."won't be long now" . . . "gotta pay your dues" . . . and then the black letters swarm before my eyes, **I WAS HERE**.

The mission is over, I call the choppers and they are on their way. Standing again I turn to my men huddled together in pairs trying to get some warmth off each other's bodies. Their weapons are slung and tucked away, their eyes now slits as they try to focus through their exhaustion. They move in slow motion, forced to contend with injuries sustained during battle. My men limp, some lean on another to get around and others work vigilantly on their brothers, trying to close or even stitch their cuts and gashes sustained in battle. Looking over them in this sad state caring for each other, I can see the amphetamines still working their dose. The pills don't allow for the adrenaline dump which gives a return to peace, they instead linger in a strain of agitation. My men are as lethal as ever. I think about my possessions that remain upstairs bound and frightened. Back at base my boss and the brass are celebrating a great victory and for them it is, but for us it is only the beginning of 100 days.

CHAPTER NINE

The Chinooks fly relaxed and high above the Afghani landscape. I can feel a slight pitch in the floor as our bird veers to avoid the occasional mountain top. The mission is over and we are returning to base for a few hours of sleep and chow. Despite our helicopter's leisurely pace, there is a fire burning inside our transport. My men still race from the extended battle. The crew of the helicopter uneasily looks to me to see if I will calm the boys, but I ignore their pleading stares. Completely alert and agitated, my men pulse from the cocktail of amphetamines the Army gave them to keep up with our nights without sleep. Their hearts still flutter from the fight and their thoughts run deep, dark, and lethal while they pace like wild animals in the confined space. They are looking for any reason to expend the remaining chemicals running through their bodies. The pills linger and consume everything and I have a front row seat as my boys become a cycle of nervous repetitious movements.

Some of them charge their pistols over and over while others sit, stand, and pace, then repeat. Several yank on the netting that covers the inside hull of the helicopter feeding their drug enforced urge to destroy. They bang fists against anything near and scream at each other over the roar of the turbo charged engine in celebration of the night's fruitful hunt. No one has slept in more than three days, but the speed they have digested gives them the power and their eyes glow red. They can't contain the electricity running through their bodies and I don't attempt to control it. The only quiet ones in the cabin are in a body bag or unconscious. Olson continues to cling to life, but his chances seem slim. Doc surrounds him like a frightened mother and fights for his life. Nova's hand is freshly bandaged and he is sleeping due to a heavy dose of pain killers.

My boys try to shake the jitters and hide from the peak they are about to descend. They still half exude an aura of calm, but no one can be cool when they are on the edge of a methamphetamine induced psychosis. Instead they become time bombs of stillness until they can no longer help themselves and eventually explode into violence. I can't compete with the chemicals and surrender to the realization that we are nothing more than simple machines, property, expendable, in every physical and mental form. We are living on borrowed time beyond genetic capabilities of the body and free will. The Army has its own agenda and pushes us further into darkness with their solution of chemical enhancement. The result is being trapped in a helicopter full of men incapable of holding a thought in their head. Every soldier rages on from his dose, but I focus my attention on the others in the cabin. We are not alone. There are spectators for tonight's entertainment.

Our mission was to find a single man and his sons and we succeeded, but we have also grabbed two full Afghani families from their homes and are bringing them with us for processing and interrogation. It is the price they pay for not telling me the whole truth and giving me reason. In this place neither probable cause nor due process exist, only men like me who rely on simple instinct. These people possibly don't know anything, but chose to lie when I questioned them and for that they are pulled out of their life, possibly forever. I watch as my men spit in their direction and our detainees huddle together in a smaller mass. They fear my men more than what is to come, but they have it wrong. I know what will happen to them. First their clothes will be taken, next a full on assault with the flash of a camera, documenting them and entering them into the database, and finally their interrogation will begin with eight hours in a squatting position.

They will be broken and will tell us everything they know and anything we ask. It will be so painful and lengthy that at some point they will wish they were back in this helicopter taking the abuse from my men. But for now they are our possessions and therefore slaves to the whims of our aggression. Under the soft red, ambient light, I see the heads of our prisoners snap back and forth from the slaps of my men, who only hit with open hands. The boys want the enjoyment of the abuse without marks advertising what has happened here. I smell the captives' fear as pistols are shoved into their mouths and my taunting mob explores a new side of their collective psyche. They are fueled by tears and shrieks of suffering and celebrate like pagans around a fire as the next man takes his turn inflicting even more damage than the previous. Watching my family behave in such an atypical manner makes them seem like strangers and yet, I feel no need to either participate or stop the show.

The old man, our prize, gazes at me in total confusion. At first glance he would seem like a benign, diseased old man, but those around him look to him with a caution beyond the normal respect they would give to an elder. He is a dangerous man, and watches his family worked over by my men with an air of satisfaction as if the abuse is a punishment he is imposing upon them for giving him up. He gives no comfort to his sons, grandsons or daughters as they take their turn in the spotlight of my men. His behavior is typical because men at war are incapable of love. There is no such thing as a passionate warrior who fights for a beating heart back home. To survive, war has to be your only true love. For many, it will be the love of their life, making all other things only a temporary reprieve from disgust.

The weathered war lord's eyes scan the inside of the bird and fix themselves on my men. His jaw drops in disbelief as he watches my boys behave like teenagers. They grab ass each other during their high and the old man looks back at me searching for the source of my power. To his people we are the ones who everyone fears. We are the ones who wear no patches and hide our faces behind beards and masks. We are invincible and worthy of the huge bounties on our heads; the body snatchers, who come in the middle of the night and from whom no one is safe. We should be worthy of the mystique that precedes us. Tonight we crushed whatever dreams this man had with lightning speed.

Despite carrying the frailty and experience of the average octogenarian in this land, he is a warrior. He barely flinches as my men yell and slap him repeatedly across the face. They sense his stature too. He possesses the look of a man who accepted his fate long ago and cannot be broken or reduced to tears even as my men wave their gun barrels and jab them into his temple. He is royalty compared to us and the more he watches the more he realizes the truth. The old man survived the Russian occupation and witnessed the horrors they inflicted on the land and now he joins the generations of lost people under the umbrella of a United States conflict. His life's work and stamina for the wars of his country should be some-thing to be admired, placed in great books and the museums of his people, but his existence is about to be washed away into the tide of our bureaucratic waste dump. I watch him still fight his war as he scrutinizes everything in the cabin.

It is unfortunate and unavoidable that my men have come to this point, but it is a natural regression. They have been treated like desert vipers for too long and have forgotten their humanity. Along the jour-ney they shed their skin in order to grow and thrive in all the things that war forces us to live. Looking at their despicable behavior, I try to pity them because every path they walk is a step in my footprint. They have allowed the war access to their soul and this place is their new home. For some there will be no road home and they'll become the next generation of monsters plowing through the desert. Watching them unfold I feel responsible. They are vampires satisfying their thirst; werewolves howling at the moon. They will never recover.

Sadly for our prisoners we take them on this journey with us. One of our captors, probably a grandson of the old man, is in his early teens and tries to shield his family from the abuse. After every hit and unnecessary taunt, he looks up at my men and stares coldly as he burns their faces into his mind. With a boyish curiosity and soldier's scrutiny he too examines the inside of our helicopter. He notes the two gunners in the middle of the bird and leans forward to see the location of the pilots. I watch him as he gathers his intelligence, but give him only a few seconds to collect his data before ordering Marti to cover his eyes. Marti complies by charging across the aisle while pulling the tape that wraps around his magazines. He steps between me and the kid and goes to work like a cowboy roping a calf. It only takes a moment. Marti steps back to examine his work and glance back to me for approval. The boy now appears back into my view with a ring of green Duck-tape around his head. I nod and Marti swings sending the kid's face into the steel floor. My men cheer and become agitated again as the punch starts a new round of abuse. I see a child bound and blinded with his head being forced face down to the floor by Marti's boot while another of my men pours water into his mouth. The act of violence receives a jittery ovation as the boy coughs and gags on the water. Enough.

I move quickly for an exhausted man and grab the soldier's fist before it reaches its mark. My face is inches from his and he understands and backs away. I stand in front of the teenager scanning the men turned beasts in front me daring one of them to make a move. Q sits at a distance, not part of the madness and slowly stands. The group hesitates and for a moment I know it can go either way. I can smell the rage and feel a dangerous smile crossing my face. The tension breaks when someone laughs. They understand what Q is capable of and aren't sure what I might do. The drugs pulsing through them and feeding their insanity are no match for real fear. Marti catches my eye and nods understanding and pats one of his brothers. Q moves a step closer as the men begin to break and return to their places of rest. Several of the boys are laughing and pounding on each other's backs. Q silently watches as their laughter recedes into nervous grumbles and aggression fades. Throughout it all the boy never utters a word and I can sense his hatred which speaks of the warrior he will become if he lives.

I'm not sure where it comes from, but I kneel in front of the blinded child and hold him in comfort. I feel him stiffen as I stroke his back in gentle circles and wonder at his thinness. Whispers and soothing sounds come from me and I rock him gently as we both experience our terrible grief. His body trembles as he struggles to hold back his sobs and loss. The boy loses his battle and his sadness escapes and fills the cabin with his wrenching cries. I hold him tighter as if he could save me and we are surrounded by silence and shame. No one moves as I gently take the tape from his eyes and suddenly there is understanding. I release my captive and scan the faces of my men, who refuse my gaze. Only Q's eyes meet mine. His secrets are safe and his pain and demons find their peace just long enough to be buried quietly.

Our journey continues and slowly one by one my men crash losing their consciousness. No one questions my moment of compassion or comfort so easily given, and I feel the monsters escape as their presence among us rushes out of the helicopter into the cold night. Their bodies are left behind and find a place on the floor among the prisoners. Exhaustion annihilates my men and they become people again.

By the second hour of our flight everyone, including the helicopter, has begun their descent. The fight is gone from all of us leaving behind the biting air causing each person to move closer to the other. Next to an M-4 sleeps a *sari* leaning in for warmth and the old man sits huddled close to a dozing Q. The boy, his face red and swollen from the tape, has finally stopped crying and buries himself deep into Marti's armpit.

I don't hunger for sleep as they do and don't need the pills or want anything they can provide me anymore. The only thing I feel is the tingling sensation of cold wind on my back and the fear of my own mind. I fight the fact that I am wandering off for moments at a time, but lose the battle as my mind drifts back into the base of my skull becoming nothing more than a voyeur to my mechanical body. The earth spins under my feet and I clench my fist in an effort to ground myself in my surroundings. It seems pointless to resist. My throbbing hand only reminds me that I am freezing and alone with ghosts.

It is a relief to distance myself from this place. To close my eyes and see lost friends on the beach under an immaculate sun with the warm sand working its way in between my toes. My boys smile as they greet the dead. Everyone looks so young and fresh as if the war has never touched us. We recline on the beach, pour drinks and share with each other our journey. Each man has a story to tell. Some speak of their death and what happens in the after-world, while others offer apologies as their guilt crushes them. It is a dream.

The day lasts long and is perfect. The ghosts continue to talk even as they grow tired and fight away heavy eyes. They yawn and sense our time is coming to an end. It is a day without closure or con-sequence. I find myself smiling at the thought of all the men lost under my command at peace and happy. I want to laugh out loud at the sight of them in a world beyond this war. The sunlight fades and my radio comes to life with my boss' voice telling me there is another mission waiting for us when we get back to base. My men and the ghosts disappear as the frigid wind dissipates my visions. My mouth an-swers the call of the radio, but my eyes still work to find the dead under the warm sun. My reverie is over.

The scene in the helicopter cabin looks like the aftermath of Gettysburg. The floor of the bird is scattered with random limbs and torsos all completely surrendered to gravity. Walking back and stepping over my men and enemies is similar to most great battles. I stir the huddle of Afghanis, tug and tighten the zip ties that hold their hands and feet together. Their faces contort to express the pinch of binds on their skin, but I continue to work trying to prevent any of them from jumping out the back as one last act of devotion to Allah. In the darkness my radio springs to life with more details of the mission still to come. My boss relays all the information needed and will be waiting for me at the landing pad to take our prisoners and push us back out again. The only words to stick in my head are "High Value Objective". I respond appropriately and calmly, but fill with rage.

Doc is on the floor dozing next to Olson, and I kick him awake harder than I should. He looks angrily at me for the disruption. I tell him there is more work to be done and he needs to hand out another round of pills for the men. We both know we are in a dangerous space that no one will bother to acknowledge. Soon the pills will become ineffective and my men no longer able to function, but we do what we are told. Duty calls. The old man offers me his hands and waits for me to tighten the restraint. I reverently take his offering as he smiles. I write a code on the back of his neck telling the interrogators that he is a valued target and return his smile. It is time. I call into my radio urging my men to stand up and ready themselves for our new assignment. I never look back at the time worn warrior again.

The only one to stir is Q, who jerks awake and promptly starts to move about kicking the boys to get them on their feet. My men slowly stand and unintentionally fall into a line to receive the day's motivation. They look like the walking dead and are in no condition to fight, but as they shuffle around cupping their hands to receive their dose like the Eucharist from Doc, I know they will. I talk into the radio briefing them on our new mission while breaking open a box of ammunition. Another line forms at my feet as my men grab bullets. They barely acknowledge my voice at the moment, but soon the pills will take hold and they will pace once again and become unable to complete a sentence or thought. I will lead them head strong and mindlessly into battle without hesitation.

We are flying over the base and will be back in this war quickly. Two small white pills rest on top of each other in my hand. I force myself to swallow despite every fiber of my body resisting the motion. The pills go down slow and grind through my throat until they are gone. No breaks. No stopping. No choice. The cycle begins. Mission two.

CHAPTER TEN

My watch reads twenty five minutes have ticked away since the roar of our helicopters left us stranded in this hostile neighborhood. We are on schedule as the dawn approaches and making good progress. The team is briefed, their lines memorized, and everyone knows their part in the play. The boys are quiet and staying off the radios as they work to shake off nerves and the chemicals that run through their bodies. The only sound is the buzzing of old street lamps like mosquito zappers that hang over our heads. Our progress is marked by a wave of aging technology as we pass under its harsh white tungsten lights. Both Q and Marti glide ahead with caution looking back to me for constant approval. I offer nothing except a jerky wave for them to move ahead. They acknowledge by turning and continuing on creating zigzag patterns in an attempt to stay out of the direct light above them. Normally, we would shoot out all the lights, but looking around at everything already shredded by war, it seems like a waste.

Out of the corner of my eye I see two dogs moving away from us through a small crack in a crumbling wall. In the air over head there are black silhouettes of a predator drone and other air assets circling over us filming every move we make. At the end of the block the smell of shit overtakes my senses as we pass next to a bombed out street now used as a sewer. The crater is the size of a VW bug and as the team passes the hole each man feels compelled to look into the abyss as if it were a gateway into the underworld. My weapon is loaded, hot, raised and everywhere as I look at a green infer-red dot through my goggles searching for an adrenaline release. I know our target is fast approaching and with each passing step I work to control the blood racing through my body.

The pills are working. My landmarks are the surrounding buildings and the street intersections that align with the aerial photo stuffed into my shoulder pocket. I know exactly where we are as we zero into the objective. Moving closer to the target building I can almost feel the energy coursing through the men. Each one of them now moves with focus as they force their bodies to step closer to the danger that lies ahead. I see their shadows as they grip and re-grip their weapons. Their guns hover completely horizontal to the ground swaying back and forth covering a sector of fire. No one bothers anymore to look down to avoid the huge fissures in the road caused by war, or do they bother to look back at me for approval.

Behind me I see the soft hue of dust rising as our boots disturb the crumbling street. The road is completely empty. The eyes in the sky tell me our flanks are clear and I pick up my pace moving up the ranks to the front of my men. The team continues forward at a constant speed and breaks into two separate elements. I end radio silence and whisper for my men to proceed. There is no need for a response, only a quickening in their step while the boys now move in pairs. Marti and his section rush off into the night to isolate the building and offer us security on the perimeter while Q's section and I move forward to our target. Faster now, I am ahead of my men moving closer to the entry and finally lean against the wall next to the front door. I take one last look at my men who scurry into their positions and hear the footsteps of Q's team as they join me. Each step sounds like the thud of a giant and I'm sure that we have awakened the people inside. I take aim at the door expecting at any moment for someone to barge out of the house with an AK-47 assault rifle, but nothing happens. The house remains quiet. Something is wrong.

I force myself to stop breathing and listen to the other side, waiting for the smallest shadow to disturb the soft candle glow that escapes from inside the house. Staring at the light creeping from the bottom of the door we are about to destroy, I stand frozen on the balls of my feet, my finger on the trigger waiting to spring into action, and still there are no signs of life. Sweat drips down my forehead and images of the house exploding expand in my mind. An elementary booby-trap detonated while my men and I work to enter is the type of thing that happens all the time. Standing there in front of the door waiting for something bad to occur, I replay the walk down the street to remember if someone was watching us make our way through the town. I picture them now, standing on roof tops, cell phone detonator in hand waiting for us to go inside so they can make their religious statement. But I'm no longer alone at the door; I have already committed my men to the mission and there is no way out.

Q's section lines up to the side of the entrance as he sets the explosive charge that will tear the front door from the house and allow our entry. My men crunch themselves into a small stack to shield from the blast. Q takes a knee just to the side and removes the adhesive from the charges. Still focused on the crack at the bottom of the door I see him work quickly showing no signs of nerves. It is his cold precision that makes him built for this life. Looking over to examine Q's work only out of habit, I see the craft of a man exhibiting his art. He is someone that is exactly where he needs to be. Q finishes setting his charge as we both inch away for cover from the explosion. Marti whispers across the radio that his section is set. Our timing so far is impeccable and I'm sure all those back in the command room are pleased with our performance.

Taking one last deep step back into the line of my men and pushing all the air out of my lungs, I feel Q bury his head between my shoulder blades. I slip my hand to his thigh and give a firm squeeze. Without hesitation and less than a millisecond later the charge sends the door into a million serrated pieces and the neighborhood is warned of our presence in their lives. The overpressure of the explosion racks our bodies, but my will pushes and I charge into the unknown. My exhaustion is a distant memory as the moment overwhelms everything else. The loss of Pete and the agony of Olson vanish in the same half second that has dominated my life for the past five years. The door disappears faster than my mind can compute and my body walks forward toward combat. The Army trains and prepares us for this first instant. Our only requirement as soldiers is to be capable of going into battle without hesitation. It is this moment that is paramount.

Breaking through the threshold, I have no idea what waits for me on the other side. Everything after is nothing more than a conditioned response to years of training and repetition. Inside the house we bathe ourselves in concussion grenades and chaos. The line I use to lead my men into the house evaporates; they now move in pairs and disperse like rats all over the structure and into each room in a single fluid motion.

They leave behind a breadcrumb trail of glow sticks to mark their location. As soon as I clear the first room, I lead another line up a flight of stairs and onto the roof where the same pattern is repeated. We move further into the house and the darkness as my heart rushes in protest. My actions are nothing more than automatic muscle movements that lead me full speed ahead despite my fears. It only takes a minute and it is over.

As the violence evaporates it becomes obvious that we are alone in the house. No shots fired, no familiar shouting of my men herding prisoners, no one calling me to examine anything, or any explosion sending us into oblivion. Despite the trembling in my hands I find my rifle has been switched to safe and already slung on my back. My pulse is still racing when I come to the conclusion that my work as a soldier is over and am now forced to become the facilitator of Standard Operating Procedures handed down to me by the Army. The radios broadcast my voice and orders signaling the start of the next phase of our operation. Rifles are replaced with cameras and explosives with electronic listening devices as we again sweep through the house, but this time with more discriminating attention. Nothing is left unturned as we look for anything that can lead us to our next objective.

Less than twenty minutes later I am walking out the front door overcome with the relief of it being over and also a growing anger. I toss hundreds of dollars back into the house for the owner to fix all the things we just destroyed. The airplanes and unmanned drones covering our approach have vanished and a lone dog begins to bark. My men regroup and prepare for our escape back to base filled with amphetamines and no chance of sleep.

Not only was my target a dry hole, but it had already been hit by some other team most likely working for a competing intelligence organization. A sense of frustration and disappointment overtakes the fear as my men bring me all the trinkets and evidence that we were beaten by another American unit. Holding my hands open, men one by one drop off the old glow sticks and markers that a previous unit used for their procedures. Q offers out his hand holding one last parting gift. I look down and see he is holding a used concussion grenade. It is just like the ones we use in my unit but with a very distinctive marking on the side. **I WAS HERE** is written in black sharpie. This guy is everywhere, but I can only manage a small grin.

The radio erupts with a transmission from my boss praising our performance and telling me how pleased our superiors are with our showing. I decide to take my time responding back and let him feel some of our anxiety for a split second. I spell out to him and anyone else listening that we were beaten to this objective by another team and the house was an empty hole. My boss trying to save face cuts me off with nervous laughter and orders us to return to base. The bang of his headset slamming on the tabletop back in the command room is proof of his true mood.

The dog has continued to bark and I see him tied in front of a darkened house. I know everyone in the town is awake and watching. His irritating yapping tells me we are not alone and should remain vigilant. Turning back to the building and focusing my attention on the surrounding structures, I see Marti and his team appear from around the corner walking in two pyramid formations preparing to lead us back to the landing zones. The men in the house exit through what is left of the front door and fall in with Marti's element. I watch as my team becomes whole again. Q appears signaling to me that the house is empty and we are ready to head back. Walking amongst the men still scanning every dark spot and rooftop, I know Q should have his own platoon by now, but his reputation precedes him and the bosses are wary. All is quiet except for the dog and our footsteps as we gather to leave the way we came.

I call back to the command room and tell anyone who still may be listening that we are coming back. The team walks much more casually, weapons still drawn and at ready but without the intensity that marked our entrance. I take a second and look back at the empty house. Every window facing the street has been shattered from the blast of our entry and where the door once hung there is now a gaping hole. Under the soft light the house almost looks at rest, but even at peace it is a testament to the toll of the war. All is as it should be when I am suddenly alerted by a shift of aggression in the barking dog.

I see Q standing alone in front of the animal, too close as it strains against its rope and loses its mind. He moves swiftly as the dog attacks and its yelp of pain stops the men. Q holds the dog in one hand by its throat and looks directly into its eyes as it snarls and struggles. Before I can move Q strangles the dog and crushes its windpipe. He gently lays the dog close to the house still tethered to its rope. Everything freezes and all are drawn to the eerie scene. Men at war can watch people die, women, children, anyone, but the killing of this dog and its simple innocence suddenly changes them.

Ben, one of our youngest, speaks first. "He was just being a dog, man. You didn't have to kill him." Q ignores those around him, takes one last look at his work, and moves through the crowd. No one stops him.

Marti yells after him, "What the fuck is wrong with you?" Q turns toward Marti and then continues on his way. "I said what the fuck is wrong with you???" and he moves toward Q, as I grab his arm.

"Let it go," I tell him low and quiet.

Marti jerks away angrily. "Someone's going to kill that crazy fuck one of these days," he spits out as he walks to the dog. "Godamnit, look at him, he's half-starved and isn't any more than an overgrown puppy. Fuck that crazy asshole." Marti strokes the dog and one more hardened veteran does the same. I see Fish, who killed easily a day ago, openly weep as he stares at the still mound of fur. For a moment weapons are ignored and danger unnoticed. We forget where we are and why, as we stand in mourning over the anonymous animal.

A helicopter flies over head and my attention is brought back to my men. I watch Q seemingly relaxed, vigilant, and waiting in the distance. "Get your men together and load up," I toss at Marti. The mood has shifted and the men reluctantly fall into place. I rejoin them and find isolation at the center of the formation. I take full responsibility for Q's actions. It was my choice to bring him back, knowing his state and in the hope that this time he'd have his shit together. Maybe he is fucking crazy and I was stupid to think that this place could heal or return what was taken. Sitting in the chopper returning from a pointless mission, I know we are all broken and mad. Q sits rigid and far away, devoid of remorse of any kind. He seems at peace knowing another mission waits. I wonder if his sleep is free of nightmares and his steps unfettered by those he's killed. Maybe Q's the lucky one.

CHAPTER ELEVEN

Our third mission is routine, a drop and snatch we had done a thousand times. We were prepped and ready after a day at base with little sleep thanks to the brutal pills given to pump us up before the dry hole mission. The men are on edge, but ready and no one on my team ever did less than what was expected. We are dropped in with the moon rising behind us. The darkness is our friend and I enter the house leading my men through the front door sure that we would be in and out quickly, but this time the enemy is waiting for me on the other side.

The muzzle of his weapon flashes from the shadows creating a strobe light effect in the small room we share. I get a shot off before falling to the ground from the impact of his bullet and know he is dead before my legs buckle under me. My knees smack the ground, rocks stinging as they burrow into my knee caps; night goggles shatter when my face slams into the dirt floor. For the first time in five years I am out of the fight. Stars and darkness fill my eyes and an unknown sense of relief suddenly swells over me. I no longer worry about anything and the crushing responsibility that I once cherished vanishes in an instant. The ground feels cool and inviting. I am ready to die and for a millisecond am at peace until pain suddenly erupts and air returns to my lungs.

I lie broken on the floor and without hesitation my men continue on with their mission. I feel the sting of my influence as their boots step over my body. Rolling to my side and into a fetal position I barely register the gunfire. Panic, terror, and excruciating pain engulf me along with the knowledge that no one is coming to help until the mission ends. I know the rules; they are my rules. I pray for Doc and watch the backs of my team disappear into the next room. Most of the men, who died under my command, spent their last moments screaming for help with their arms extended, grasping at air. The last image they would see were the backs of their brothers fulfilling their duty. The reality of what I have done is an avalanche suffocating me.

Nothing prepared me for these seconds of agonized torture. The gun fire finally stops and all I want is to not die alone. I struggle to keep from screaming for help as the fear takes a stronger hold. The many men I left to die until a mission was complete encircle me. I hear their voices echoing, begging me to save them. Each wail sends excruciating waves of throbbing hurt through my body and when darkness claims me I welcome the escape. According to the Army the operation is a success.

The night's mission is over and I find myself conscious and back at base. I stand in my team's dressing room, drenched in sweat with only my will keeping screams at bay. I am frozen in pain and can't breathe. Cheating death has a way of sucking the air and fight right out of you. With each half agonized breath, I struggle to grab air in a panting gasp and pray my quick slam of pain killers can give me some relief. I am alone and understand I have to sit to finish the post mission shit, but I need a moment to get up the nerve. This is how Tuff Hedeman must have felt, knowing he was going to ride Bodacious again, or Evel Knievel after his jump in London. I can do this. Slowly bending my knees and dropping my hands to grab the bench I try to take the weight off my legs. It is the kind of pain that tells you it's not going to be okay. The wooden slats of the bench dig into my thighs as a welcome distraction. Finally on my ass, I take a rattling intake of air and nearly black out. Jesus.

The thought of eternal damnation is foremost in my mind. Every inch of me hurts. I grit my teeth and reach to release my armor straps. With the sound of tearing Velcro and a hollow thump, the life-saving Kevlar falls to the floor. I can breathe a little easier, but agony pulses through me. Chills climb down a sweat soaked spine and my body shakes. Perspiration pours from my face like tears despite the freezing room and as I wipe it away the dirt and grit feel like sand paper against raw skin. If I hold position maybe the burning that rips through me will stop.

I wait for the drugs to kick in and examine my gloved hands closely as my body pulses. The hard plastic that covers the knuckles is scuffed and cracked from abuse. The trigger finger is worn through exposing thick black muck under my over-grown fingernail. I am fighting hard, swallowing my guts, and tell myself I am glad to be alone. In the time it took me to get checked out by a doctor, the boys dropped their equipment off and went back to the house to get some much needed sleep. I can't blame them and would do the same, but am surprised by my sobs ricocheting against the metal walls. Feeling sorry for myself is something new for me and I struggle to shove down my moans and suck it up. Trap already cleared me for duty despite two broken ribs and a bruised lung. I'd laugh if I didn't think it would kill me.

Only my extreme pain keeps the demons away today. I can hear them in the distance fighting for my attention and as always they are patient. I focus on Marti's equipment hanging close to me. In the center is a cross made of 2X4s holding his armored vest off the floor to allow it to dry and be easily accessible for the next mission. Beside his Kevlar is a weapon with the barrel pointed to the ground and his helmet suspended by nails. The boots unlaced are below and waiting. Close to Marti's armor, Fish's equipment hangs in the exact same manner and next to it the cross that once held Olson's equipment stands empty, disrupting the order that holds the room together.

Not now. I avert my eyes and scan the room for escape. Two more vacant spaces, stark crucifixes scream the names of those who once stood beside me. I should be thinking of the men we lost this trip, but instead I picture the area where my gear is stored cleared of any remnant of me. The bosses would be forced to give Q his promotion and he would take the team. One mad man takes over for another. It would be as if I never existed. Dark thoughts are creeping in with the drugs. The pain is lessening, but my fear is growing.

Two years ago I felt alive. Hell, two weeks ago my heart was in the fight. The last time I was shot, I laughed and demanded a cigarette from my men. I made a spectacular show of it and hobbled around the objective taunting the captured enemy soldiers. My men applauded by shaking their heads in disbelief; their grins were my standing ovation. I have learned many things since then. Things that make my feet feel heavy and my back ache. Today I am tired and old.

Shifting my weight to find comfort, I stifle an emerging scream. Pain shoots through me, knives slashing the soft parts leaving agony in their wake.

My vest lies at my feet and the dark burnt smudge made by a bullet colliding with the armor is visible. I stop cold, lean over despite the grip on my chest, and touch the bullet. It looks more like a small clump of mud than a round from an AK-47. I circle the rough edges of the bullet with my finger. It hit right above the magazine pouches, three inches below where my left nipple would be. If the bullet had been over an inch more to the side it would have missed the plate altogether and gone into my ribs. I am lucky to be alive, but have no sense of relief as the images of the night replay in my head.

The empty crosses watch as I hit my chest with a closed fist hard, hoping the body pain will save me from their souls and bring me back to the numbness that has allowed me to thrive in this war. The self-inflicted torture takes me to my knees. I rock on the floor attempting to stop the gut wrenching sounds coming out of me and suddenly Hartman is there. I weep at the sight of my long dead friend, who smiles and reaches out his hand in comfort. No. Not now, not here. I squeeze my eyes tight, but can smell the place, Qatar, Iraq during the rainy season. I was a squad leader in the early days of the war and we were in some back street moving towards our objective. The steady rain had flooded everything, overflowed the sewers. Hartman and I were slopping through the floating shit and I can hear the guys behind me struggling to stay on their feet and avoid falling into the slop as I turn into another shit filled alley.

A black figure stands alone in the center of the street. I take quick aim at the form's head. My heart pounds as I realize it is just a kid, twelve at the most. His eyes are wide, his mouth open and panting in fear. His rifle at waist level is fixed on me and we stand frozen, face to face. If he wanted the boy could have taken me out when I turned the corner, but he didn't. The barrel of his AK-47 trembles along with his body and his tears reflect the ambient light of the alley.

I step to the side, out of the way of his barrel and order my men to take cover away from the boy. As they retreat, I slowly walk around the rifle and attempt to coax the weapon out of his hand. Hartman stays with me, his weapon at ready pointed at the kid in case I need cover. The child is so small that the water comes up to the middle of his shins. I try my best broken Arabic and tell him to drop the weapon and go home in the most soothing voice I could muster, but he stands his ground staring straight ahead his eyes fixed at nothing. I am surprised by his courage; in all my deployments I have never seen anyone hold their ground against us. I realize this child is dangerous, but move closer within arm's reach.

Slowly reaching towards him to grab the weapon my mind registers something familiar. It is the slightest of noises and reminds me of my grandmother's screen door flapping in the desert gusts of the El Paso desert. It is almost an unnoticeable disruption that will change everything. I don't want to do what is needed and I hesitate before my muscles finally react. The creaking sound is the retention spring of the trigger as the boy starts to squeeze. I answer, but it is too late. He gets a round off before my bullet blows a hole in his face. He is so small. Completely still, knees locked back, the boy's blank face is still fixed down the alleyway. I glance to see what he was looking at so intently and at that moment both Hartman and the child fall to the ground as if they are reflections of the same mirror.

Staring at the boy face down in a puddle of water, the back of his head blown away, his arms floating, I am frozen with the realization of what my compassion has done. Doc is running and sliding into Hartman who still lies face down in a shallow puddle. He turns him over and begins sharp mechanical movements, but they slow and eventually stop. Completely soaked, Doc looks at me expressionless. I know that my friend is dead and my choices killed him. We leave him and the child in the filthy water until the mission is complete.

Hartman. I had pushed his memory deep, and thought I learned the lesson well and here he is again, laughing at me and calling me weak. Blank eyes surround me, dead children and weeping women. I gasp with the pain and horror of the memory, but my tears make no difference. Hartman and the boy's deaths stopped nothing and were barely a sentence in a bureaucrat's report.

I'm not sure how long I am gone this time revisiting a memory I hoped to never experience again. The pain killers are working along with my exhaustion and I find myself still alone and shivering in the empty room. I slowly pick up my armor and reach for my weapon, hang them in their home and unlace my boots. A glance at my watch tells me I have only hours before my next mission. Everything is off and nothing feels right. Groggy from the pills, but free of the unspeakable pain, I stumble toward my boys with the shadows of the dead weighting my every step. Let me sleep dear God, free of memory and nightmare. Hartman's laughter follows me as Mike's words taunt, "Crying like a little girl, Cevera, gotta pay your dues, soldier. . ."

CHAPTER TWELVE

My eyes slowly open and for a moment I don't register the freezing night wind that cuts through me or my soreness. I choose to look at my watch rather than acknowledge the man tapping my shoulder and realize that despite the uncontrollable shivering of my extremities, I have slept for an hour and a half, my longest stretch of undisturbed sleep in as long as I can remember. Shrugging off the weight of comatose sleep and pain killers, I begrudgingly turn to the crew member still trying to wake me. "Ten minutes," he mouths, while he holds out his hands, fingers spread and covered by huge arctic-type gloves, in front of my face. I simply nod and shove my own hands deeper into my armpits in an effort to warm them against the sub-zero blasts that accompany our open helicopter. As it screams along less than 100 feet above the ground I wonder if I actually heard the crewman's words over the turbines or my imagination gave him a voice. Another mission is about to begin and I ache in pain and am completely exhausted.

Two of the chopper's crewmen hover over their 20 millimeter canons. They hold their ground against the unrelenting swerves of the bird and icy wind while it banks around tall trees and buildings. Both men stand like linebackers, hungry and poised to strike on either side of the open doors. Their eyes, glowing green from their goggles, make me certain that upon arrival these men will release their full concentration upon the unsuspecting world below. I am relieved to see their intensity because my men barely cling to their sanity and are going to need all the help they can get.

I sit up from the freezing metal floor and force myself to take off the parka that protects me from the arctic winds cutting through the cabin. Urging my frozen hands to cooperate, I switch on my head lamp and re-examine the picture of the man we are going to *retrieve*. I announce "Ten minutes," in a radio monotone and look over the pile of bodies that sleep in the middle of the floor. Like a large animal fighting its instinct to just roll over and die, the mass slowly starts to move. Each figure stays low and close

to the man next to him in an effort to shield themselves from the cold air, but it is pointless. There
isn't any comfort in this world or this line of work.
Neither the picture attached to the inside of my forearm nor the words I used to brief the mission mean
anything to me. Even as I speak the words, "High
Value" and "Hard Cell", I feel my voice falling on deaf
ears. The operational pace has stolen our adrenaline
and no one cares for anything other than getting out
of the cold and sleep. I barely listen to my own voice
as I deliver the plan to my men and see that numbness has overtaken all of us.

I force myself to stand for the first time since
boarding the helicopter and struggle to get my balance as the blood rushes into my extremities. Each
step toward the back of the cabin is accompanied by
shivers and the tingling sensation of a limb in sound
sleep. The pain awakens me. My ribs throb and every time I clinch my fist I pulse with agony. I pass the
pile of stragglers still working to wake up and kick
various lumps in the mass to further coax my men
from their peace. Medals are going to be handed out.
My boys performed flawlessly during this deployment with hundreds of kills and several dozen pris-

oners. I acknowledge their collective achievements, but my mind remains on our present purpose.

Jenkins, the newest member of my team, sits up and wipes his eyes. Although it is too dark for him to see, I smile in false approval. He looks at me hovering over him and my thoughts wander to the pit bull he and his wife bought before this deployment. I was working late one Friday night and he showed up with his wife and dog in the locker room. I wanted to laugh when he talked to his dog like it was a baby, but stayed quiet and still at my desk to hear their conversation. Jenkins showed his wife and dog his equipment and explained to her how nervous he was about his first deployment. His wife held back tears and responded with words of encouragement. He reacted to his wife with a choked up "I love you" and a hug. Listening to them discuss their dreams and fears, I was surprised at the openness of their marriage and decided not to interrupt their last moments together. Now, Jenkins, with his knees pulled tightly to his chest and his hands buried in his armpits, looks more like a junkie going through withdrawals than a warrior.

I feel sorry for him. I know he probably misses his wife and dog. I think about him hugging his wife in the locker room and how I heard the love between them from the next room. I know he has no idea why we are going after our target and the look of total confusion on his up-turned face makes me feel even more sympathy for him. He killed his first man at close range this trip and I was sure that made his home feel very far away. I believe I should apologize to his wife. The man that held her that night in the locker room is dead and will never touch her the same way again.

I am responsible. I instinctively place my hand on his shoulder and watch as Jenkins straightens his back and regains a proud posture. Before my feelings are exposed I quickly return his shivering grimace with a nod and walk toward the back of the helicopter. This cold dark hole is not a place for doubts or memories. I take one last, good look at the guy in the photo taped to my arm and think about the man as if he is already gone. I am alerted that positions on the ground have changed. The enemy has attacked and American soil taken in this foreign land. I scan the dazed bunch around me and regret refusing Doc's offer to give two more doses of amphetamines. He sought me out before we boarded the birds to start the boys on their bi-weekly rations of speed. The pills are supposed to help us cope with the "operational tempo", but instead, these supplements have plagued our unit with addictions and depression. Thinking of the men jittery and pacing around aggressively seems far more appealing at this particular moment than watching them struggle to keep their eyes open. If I lose a man tonight it will be my fault.

Swimming through my doubts I walk closer to the open ass of our ride and see another crewman sitting on the ramp looking at the cloud of dust that trails our passage. His legs dangle off the side as his head scans from left to right. I lean forward and grab his collar, but he doesn't turn to look at me. Dropping to a knee I too stare into the night sky. Looking up through the rotor blades that spin over my head I struggle to examine the moonless black that surrounds us. I am looking into the abyss and think how easy it would be to simply let myself fall. No more battles or dead men. "Q", I speak into my radio. He responds with, "We're up and ready," in his deep voice as if he is expecting my transmission. He too was alerted at what awaits us.

I drop my night vision goggles over my eyes and the world beyond my reach is revealed to me. I look back into the trail of dust and see Q's helicopter following closely behind. I picture the other half of my team struggling to stand and prepare themselves for their work. The other Chinook bobs and weaves through tree tops as it seems to struggle to keep up while the rotor blades emitting static electricity give the trailing bird two green halos. It banks hard and the nose dips as if to bow and acknowledge my inspection, but anything showing reverence to me leaves a bad taste in my mouth.

Weapon ready, I stand up and grab one of the thick ropes that will deliver us into combat. As I pull on the rope I glance back into the cabin and see the men standing and stretching as turbulence suddenly jerks everyone violently. My feet leave the steel floor and land with the arches of my feet on the lip of the ramp. Still holding the rope I look down and see the tips of my boots hanging off the edge while the ground rushes below me in a blur. Suddenly, we are over a small city.

The streets are littered with large concrete barricades the Army had placed to stop the flow of traffic. I can smell the huge stagnant pools that our bombs created as they destroyed the water and sewer mains. Rusted-out car hulks and the occasional destroyed Humvee mark the sight of a former battlefield. I have been here before. Out there somewhere is the Hedetha Dam and my last memory of Mike. Two years ago in this very same city, I carried him off the battlefield after a night long firefight. He took two rounds to the chest while he was leading us across the dam into the fight. Away from the fight I laid him on the ground. He gave no parting words, only a smile of approval and then left me.

The helpless city unravels beneath my feet as the helicopter races to deliver me and my contribution to the devastation. My eyes are flooded with images of destruction and war that will never be allowed on American television and I am frozen as the dying city exposes itself. "Joe?" the radio breaks its silence and the moment, "You think this is a door on the North side of building 202?" Marti asks. "If it is, that's where I would like to enter."

"No," I quickly respond, "forget the target, Intel reports dozens of enemy fighters on the ground. Diving into fire tonight. Follow my lead."

"One Minute," a crewman cuts in on the radio. I turn in to see all my men standing in two single lines on both sides of the cabin. Marti steps onto the ramp next to me and begins examining the rope the men on his side will use to slide down. He looks to me and nods as the crew chief holds up the sign for thirty seconds. The helicopter banks hard and starts to slow down, eventually coming to a complete stop. The ground seems so far below me and for a split second I see myself falling. Over a hundred drops and I'm still afraid. The crew chief pulls the pins and the ropes as if in slow-motion, unwind and fall to the earth. I take my final step and the last thing I see as the momentum of my descent spins are my men in line waiting to take their plunge into the world below. I know they will all follow me to the ends of the earth because this is where we belong. We are the cavalry come to save the day, and when all hope is lost are ready to give whatever is asked.

I am on the ground once again like so many times before, holding a gun. Things are slowed as even time struggles to keep up with my men as they follow me into the fight. The subtle recoil into my shoulder is the only reminder that I am pulling the trigger. Eye into my sight, I can feel the displacement of bullets swim by my face, but this is no time for hesitation. My enemy has shown their determination to stand and fight and I will oblige them.

There is a pocket of energy displaced at the exact point where a bullet ends its journey. Like a rock falling into a calm pond it sends a ripple of chaos away. It is a portal that opens when my targets hit the ground. I see men with guns and run right for them. I am the Kamikaze ready for what happens next and surrendering to the will of the war. Running deeper into the gunfight my men are close by my side as they always have been and I feel their warmth.

The recoil of my rifle on my shoulder and more fall down. There is no thought involved, nor do any choices present an alternative to the outcome, just the brain's instinctual electro-chemical process tuned by countless acts of repetition. Our target is either long gone or dead, the building, scorched and destroyed. The firefight escalates, and the streets fill with our enemies dead and cast aside. My plans are forgotten as we move quickly into the center of the conflict. The men understand the shift without fear or regret. Their mouths hang half open and their eyes focused to the front. Any advancement is accented by the occasional pause to look at our flanks and update into the radio. I feed them instruction and they adjust accordingly.

I can hear the panic and shouting of my enemy while they bicker at each other from the shadows. I feel their fear as they realize victory is slipping into my hands. I call my men back into the fight and they answer with a hail of gunfire rushing past me to cover the advance. I am calm. My heart beats only expending enough energy for me to pull the trigger. I'm running fast when I pass a group of soldiers huddled together in a dark corner waiting their turn to die. Dumb luck placed them in the center of this gunfight. I shift my advance away from them, but one is hit by a stray bullet and spins around from the force finally coming to rest on his side, eyes dead. I am no savior.

The fact that other lives are spared is only a biproduct of the desire to keep my men alive. I don't look back nor do I expect any assistance from those we came to rescue through the fight. My actions don't stir anything except the vacant look of shock as they wait their turn to meet their end. They wait for death as we run towards it. We are heroes, only because we hunger for what they fear and were trained to embrace death. This is our victory tonight.

I find myself pushing ahead further toward the enemy line. Soon I can see their faces and smell their sweat from behind their makeshift barricades. I am well within their range and a wave of gunfire erupts. I become their only target and still I move ever forward as fear breaks their ranks. My men and their guns are relentless as the enemy begins to turn and run. Rage fills me as my bullets find the backs of their retreating heads. Our onslaught never waivers and our enemy shrieks as they feel their deaths approach. Some simply drop to the ground and pray as the gunfight evolves into an execution. I move back as my men surge forward leaving nothing but ghosts in their wake. Finally relaxing, I take a deep breath of the cold night air as the gunshots continue to echo around me. No one ever escapes. The dead are left, the injured suffer, and those who survive are seared with the images of this place.

It is our frustration that fuels us now. A frustration I can feel in my body and the bodies of my men. From Doc's sluggishness to rope out of the helicopters to Marti's limp at a possible broken ankle; Q's descent into madness, and the cracking oozing scabs on my knuckles caused by beating any resistance from prisoners, tell the story of who we have become. We are paying the bills, but in war, money has no value. Pain and suffering are the only currency here. I no longer hear the moans of the dying or the calls to God. The mission is complete. This is victory and I am surrounded by the men who work only to survive to see another dawn regardless of the cost.

CHAPTER THIRTEEN

My team of operators and I began this deployment hungry and have gorged ourselves in every facet of this ragged country. The rollercoaster ride that was the last month of my life has been labeled a total success by the Army and those who decide such things. Yet the death toll is rising. After every mission I count my soldiers as they leave the target buildings heading back to base, and the final number I reach is always two less than it should be.

Shifting to my side, I look at the rows of bunks and it feels like I'm standing between two mirrors and seeing a never ending repeating reflection. Each is occupied with either a man or his gear identical to my bunk. My hope is that we will not have to pack anymore belongings and ship them back home. The odds are not in our favor, but it isn't these thoughts that keep me awake. It is what waits when I finally close my eyes. My watch tells me I have been lying on my back for over an hour and the window for sleep is slowly closing. Sleeping during the day has never been easy. I'm running on fumes, but my nervous mind keeps telling me to get up and go back to work. It's becoming harder to hold on and hide the cracks in my veneer. The nightmares are frequent and terrifying.

Attempting to keep the demons at bay, I force myself to remember the great times shared with the men sleeping around me, but everything is quickly cluttered together. Blood and booze. Suffering and smiling. Killing and fucking. Images and faces rush ahead of my consciousness coupled with a sense that my days are numbered. A lifetime comes and goes only to be replaced with another. Africa, Pakistan, Iraq, Afghanistan, Iran, Haiti all are warped and wrapped together into a flashing chaos without order or reason. I measure my breathing and cover my eyes with an arm, but the darkness makes the graphics intensely vivid. I am starting to sweat. Deep breaths. Slow the heart and thoughts. Tonight will be dreamless, I tell myself and reach for nothingness. I can feel my racing mind hesitate while the weight of my hands becomes light. The tension in my shoulders relaxes and the pain in my ribs floats away.

I seek complete surrender, everything now heavy and warm. In the space between unconsciousness and awareness my mind struggles to gain a foothold and then I am gone.

I wake up with Charlie's last whispered words hanging in the air, "It's hard because I'm left handed." A gun shot from long ago rings in my ears. I gasp, sitting up in panic, seeing the brain matter, blood, and spinal fluid dancing like a lava lamp sliding down the wall behind his face. Gulping for air, I look around the room to see if I have disturbed anyone. No one is moving. I close my eyes and try to force myself back to sleep, but I know it is pointless. No sleep tonight as the vision of an ancient city and Charlie's suicide hold in my mind's eye. The memory is stronger than reality and it is futile to fight it. Let the past run its course. The city is burning.

The boys and I were sent as one of the first to the city to help launch the counter offensive in 2004. I remember flying in our Blackhawks toward the fight, all of us hanging out the door watching the traffic jam of Hummers and Bradleys in their mass exodus of the city. The Marines a week earlier decided to arrest almost every man in the city and then careless-

177

ly let them go; one of the great blunders of this war. Fallujah, Iraq erupted into a violent wave of chaos in protest to the U.S. presence in their lives. The Marines retreated and the military answered by sending almost everyone in the region to quell what was dubbed by the press as an insurgent revolt.

As the soldiers beneath us ran away, we prepped for battle, readying ourselves for anything once we hit the ground. I only took one radio and expected to be mowed down by gunfire while making my way down the ropes. Charlie was to be the last man out of the helicopter. This allowed the leader to be left among the survivors once we began our assault. It all happened in reverse.

Most of us made it to the safe house. The city was tearing itself apart just outside the door. The boys screamed situational updates at each other across the room and completed every sentence with the pull of a trigger. I felt the energy shift in all of them, and even though I had not looked outside to survey the situation, I knew it was dire. We needed to escape and then Charlie, our leader, shot himself.

I froze. Forgotten was the burning city and the raging crowd outside our front door, there was only

Charlie. The image of that moment, long buried, is all I see in the darkness. I watch as life struggles to stay inside his body. His cheeks are clinched while he violently exhales causing spit and blood to bolt out of his puckered lips staining his clothes and mixing with the open wound on his left forearm. I lie in my bed suffocating under the horror of the images. The gun refuses to fall to the ground, but remains pressed under his chin and the smell of burning meat fills this room of sleeping men as the memory takes hold.

Charlie killed himself and no one noticed or asked why. The rest of the men in the safe house continued to fight for survival focused only on what lay beyond the crumbling walls. This had kept us alive so far. My leader lay awkwardly on his side, his hands pulled tight into his chest twitching like an epileptic, and his eyes focused on me. They glazed over and a familiar blankness overtook his once expressive face marking the end of our friendship. He was gone. My grief and loss for my friend must wait, and maybe is still waiting, but at that moment the only thing that came to mind was how hopeless our situation was. The man on the ground was the lone rival to contest my position as team leader and he just blew his own head off. I was now responsible for getting the men surrounding me out of the mess we were ordered into. Time to get back to work.

I called Doc over while I took Charlie's radio from his back and pocketed his unused magazines. Ripping the Velcro on his shoulder, I grabbed his call sign placard as well and watched Doc franticly go to work on the dead. Doc slowed as he pieced together what Charlie had done and looked to me dazed in confusion. Still holding the gun to his head my friend continued to broadcast his last wish. I took the weapon and ordered Doc back to his post.

My entire team was split into two separate elements, both on the verge of being overwhelmed by the enemy. I told Q to get ready to move. "Get all the boys on the roof" and was amazed at how calm my voice sounded. Marti heard the order and I responded to him by pointing to the ceiling. He got up from the hole in the wall he was shooting through and started to remove explosive charges from his pack. I left him examining the best way to blow an opening in the roof without bringing the entire house down upon us and made a call to headquarters for air support. I hoped that the noise of planes overhead would be enough to disperse the horde outside.

The response was quick and expected, "Kilo Alpha 12, there is no air support at this time." We were alone and all eyes were on me.

"Marti, you still alive?" I roared over the chaos.

"So far," he responded.

"I want those charges set in two minutes," I hoped Q had heard.

"I'm on it," he interrupted before I could make the call. Crawling on my belly to the outer wall, I saw the crowd had doubled in size. Men, women, and children mixed in with armed men wearing black wraps around their heads signifying that they were Taliban. Spit and rocks mixed with gunfire were aimed at our safe house. I knew it was only a matter of time before the angry mob was replaced by a trained military force that would leave us outnumbered and without supplies. "I'm ready," Q's steady voice interrupted my panic, "everyone's still here and we got enough ammo to get us to night fall."

I looked to Marti. "I'm good too, except for Kurt Cobain over there." I was immediately angered by

Marti's response to Charlie's death, but did not respond.

"On my mark, I want the charges going simultaneously and then start barricading everything against the front wall to the crowd." I broadcast the countdown to detonation for the entire team. Everyone got low, tucking their heads as the charges went off and the room filled with dust and rubble. The windows of the house vanished and revealed the actual size of the mob outside. I heard them cheering and chanting for another blast to finish us off as the boys scrambled throwing chairs and rugs against the front door and wall.

Q cracked the front door and leaned a copy of the Koran outside of it. "See if they like shooting that," he shouted with a grin.

"Get everybody on the roof and keep it quiet," I ordered not ready to be amused. First out of the hole was Marti, and as quickly as his feet levitated out of sight his hand reappeared ready to pull the next man up. One by one they disappeared. Last was Doc dragging Charlie to the opening, "Leave him." Doc didn't turn to face me, but reluctantly laid Charlie on the ground in the center of the room and made his escape through the hole.

With my team on the roof I was ready to enact my plan for escape. Marti came back with his report. "Hey man, everybody is on the roof staying out of sight."

"Have them push away from here as far as they can and get ready to get me out in a hurry," I shouted. "Q" I continued, "try to figure out how to get everyone down, but wait until evening prayer. Remember make sure everyone stays out of sight."

"What are you doing?" Marti asked and I didn't answer.

It was just me and Charlie. I drug him to my corner and laid him on his side. I said my last good-bye to my friend and got on my knee and surveyed the crowd. "I'm going to see how much fight this mob has," I whispered to myself and answered Marti's question. My sight found a man holding a weapon and addressing the crowd. He was screaming his hatred and pointed his rifle angrily at the house with the syllables of each word. I shot him and watched the crowd gasp in horror. Three fell to the ground in the first burst. The mob wailed and scattered returning fire. I hid behind Charlie. "Sorry bro," I spoke to his limp body. He would have hated what I was doing. Charlie was a man who moonlighted as an amateur bodybuilder and gazed at his body in the mirror for hours. He was probably one of the vainest people I'd ever met; and now, he was nothing more than a shield against the war trying to get in.

Glass and parts of the wall bounced all over me and the body. As the shooting tapered off I got back on my knee and took three more men. The frenzied crowd surged and returned my volley. Spooned against Charlie I waited for someone to try and rush the front door. "You missed me!" I screamed and heard the guys on the roof laughing. I popped up in time to see two men charging the door. I waited until the first one was completely in before I shot him in the face. Covered in the blood of his running mate, the second man hesitated long enough for me to end his life. I turned my attention back to the crowd and took three more of the enemy.

I felt my friend's body jerking from the bullets and knew protection was running out. I crawled over to the two men just killed and picked one of them up like a sack of grain and threw him out the door. I heard the crowd gasp and realized they were moving closer. Getting back to my spot I peered over the window and shot another three in the legs. Those in front were backing off even as they returned fire. I felt the first bullet make it through Charlie hitting my back armor plate and knew it was time to leave. "Marti" I shouted, "I'm coming to you, get ready."

I dumped all my empty magazines over Charlie's body and wrenched a grenade from his vest. Pulling the pin, I buried it under his back making sure the spoon stayed intact. I did the same thing under the other body in the room. I called to Marti telling him I was on the way. His hands came down through the hole to yank me up. With a quick tug on the pin, I held the spoon from my last grenade and made a frantic run across the room. With the windows gone the enraged population could see me rushing for Marti's dangling arms. The entire structure erupted as they took aim at me crossing the opening in the wall. I expected to be wounded at any moment as they hit the house with everything they had. Looking up at the hands that hung down for me, I threw my last grenade at the door and jumped up toward the hole. I had five seconds before it exploded.

One Mississippi, both feet off the ground and my arms stretched for Marti's. I grabbed his hands and he clenched tight. *Two Mississippi*, my head above the ceiling, I saw the sky above me as Marti and Olson pulled me through. The jagged edge of the hole scraped my thighs as if the house wanted to suck me back in. *Three Mississippi*, I broke free from its hold and on my hands and knees crawled away. I screamed for my men to run and move to the next roof. They did and never looked back. *Four Mississippi*, on my feet I ran in a crouched posture certain that I wouldn't make it in time. *Five Mississippi*, I saw my men on the next building over. I wasn't going to make it.

The roof beneath my feet jerked violently from the explosion of the first grenade. I attempted to regain my balance and still make progress off the roof as the next two grenades blew. I could hear the sound of crumbling stone and mortar behind me before I rolled to a stop and heard the crowd below in a total state of panic. For a moment I simply stopped.

I was on my back on the next building with the blue sky overhead and listened while the safe house cried in protest and eventually succumbed to gravity.

The sounds of people frantically going through the rubble looking for loved ones was almost a lullaby, but the echoes of gunfire in the distance eventually brought me back from my trance state. I peeked over the side at the destruction beneath me; the once enraged mob had vanished and turned into a meandering dazed herd. Sinking back out of sight I thought about what could possibly have survived the blasts. Charlie was most likely completely gone, reduced to stains on rocks buried beneath layers of debris. It was not a proper burial but the only one I could provide.

I pulled out a smashed box of cigarettes and lit a smoke. I noticed that all eyes had turned to me. They were waiting and I did not hesitate to accept my new role. "Start cross loading your ammo and make sure all radios are up, we are going to be here for one hour." The boys began counting the rounds they had left in their magazines and ensuring that everyone had the same amount. Once that was done some of the men pulled security while others took naps. No one mentioned Charlie or challenged my imposed position among them. It was as if they had already forgotten what they lived through and who we lost, but I hadn't.

The random explosions and bombs being dropped all around us had become nothing more than crickets chirping through the night. As long as the fight was not on our front door it seemed no one cared about the violence surrounding us. I sat on the roof looking over the sky line at the random flames spreading across the city, and thought about what it meant to lead these men. I knew I could do the job with honor and distinction. Mike would have loved this and I hear his easy laugh.

The sun was setting and the red sky overhead began to fill with stars. The plumes of smoke from the burning buildings were columns in the darkening sky as if they held up the heavens above. The birth of the moon and its glow silhouettes the city against the celestial backdrop. The whole world was fading away along with the sun. The city was on fire and was one of the most beautiful things I have ever seen.

They used to call this combat fatigue and I chuckle to myself at the irony. Fatigue is right, sick to shit of the past fucking with me. The room is still and I force myself to become a part of this scene of sleeping men, almost as if I belong. I focus on calming my heart and my trembling hands. I only know how to do two things in this life well: survive and fight. I require both now. I'm not sure if I can survive these night terrors and battle these episodes, these indulgences. Once they seemed to be a passing event like the season. Now they are crippling my abilities and find me wishing for any kind of escape. I look to my men down the row, most sleep with their backs to me because of the light breaking into the room. They need their sergeant as much as I need them and depend on me to take them through the gauntlet and get them home to live their lives. I know this fact foremost and never need to be reminded, but I'm not sure how to hang on anymore.

I want my pills and roll to the edge of the bed giving myself permission to take my pain killers early. The shock of the icy floor to my feet brings me completely out of my dream state and I take a double dose for luck. The room is still and relief spreads over me when I recognize that no one fully knows about my situation. I can't allow anything to cast doubt on me or my abilities to lead the unit. I owe it to my boys to stay strong and capable to keep them safe, but I'm not sure anymore if I am capable. Hearing their deep breaths of sleep gives me comfort and for a moment I sit listening to the soothing rhythm of their peace. It is them I serve now and no one else.

CHAPTER FOURTEEN

I've lost count of the missions. We are deep into this one after 24 hours of rest at base. No escape from the horrors that I have committed or the lives I have lost. I scan our destruction. Seventeen seconds and a life time is reduced to a pile of rubble. I hear Marti interrogating the man and woman of the house in the front room; his interpreter mimics perfectly the inflections of Marti's yelling. The couple ignores our demands for answers and responds with cries and pleas. The husband begs to get a robe to cover his wife and shield her aging body from our eyes, but her humiliation is part of the process. Strolling by the woman, I notice blood running from her head, probably caused by our explosive entrance. She looks dazed as if lost at sea, allowing the blood to run down her face and finally into her mouth. The drops that escape her nightgown pool on the floor next to her bound feet. Swaying in every direction, she tries to gain her bearing and finally her eyes fix on me as if I can make this all go away.

Two minutes ago everyone in this house was in a peaceful sleep. Two minutes ago this was one of the nicest houses I had ever seen in Afghanistan, but now it is like all the others, a crumbling shell scarcely capable of supporting its own weight. I hear my men executing their jobs before the dust has time to settle. The cupboards squeal in protest as they are pulled from the walls and a chorus of dishes and glass crash to the ground. The boys will clear all shelves and drawers searching for the magical item that will move us to the next target and closer to ending this war. Every window in the house was broken from the overpressure of our explosion and with every step I feel glass and debris crutching under my boots. Walking down the hall I run my hand along the tile wall, my gloves snag on the fresh cracks. I have lived this moment hundreds of times. These stress fractures have become my signature in braille.

Like the rest of the house the last room I enter is completely turned upside down. Even though everything is out of place and thrown into the center of the floor I can still tell it is a child's room. The shelves, like the posters of random sports figures, are hung in the low middle of the walls. There is a mixture of toys and tools tossed into a central mess without reverence or consideration for their owner. I am alone in the dark and even though I hear all the screaming from the front room as the interrogation continues, it feels like everyone is a thousand miles away. Hovering over the pile and throwing a bed frame against the wall my flash light finds two feet protruding from the bottom of the mound of junk. One foot still holds onto a sandal. Reluctantly I remove the mattress that covers the rest of the body.

It's a typical scene, but my stomach tightens. His clothes reflect the boy's awkward age with a robe too large and pants too short. Everything is mismatched. Not quite a child and not yet a man with feet too big for the body, the mustache too thin. I kneel and dust off the debris that litters the body revealing the adolescent frame lost somewhere in-between and above its tomb of trash. The hands twitch as the brain refuses to die, but I know it will be over soon and feel the energy escaping the two bullet holes in his chest. Soon hands that grab at air will freeze and feet which once ran in joy will stop their struggle. Pulling my knife I gently cut off the vest that drapes the torso. I run my hands around the body and along the back to make sure there are no booby traps to detonate the two grenades the child wears as accessories. Finding nothing, I hug the body to cut away the vest and grenades. The blood shifts inside the torso and I feel one last breath on my neck like a whisper. It sends a chill over my body and I pull back in panic for a moment. I search the young face for any sign of life, but the child's memories and soul are gone.

The story of his death is told through the blood splatter on the wall and floor. I see my men enter the room and perceive an enemy with weapons. Less than a full second later the kid is bouncing off the wall as two bullets propel his body backwards. They drag him to the middle of the room and he is forgotten, buried with trash as they search for intelligence material. My men are in and out in less than two minutes. The boy dies in three.

I know someone put these grenades in his hands and dressed him in the vest long before we ever made our way into this house and I refuse to let that secret die in this room. I scan the area for anything else that may be contraband. The age of the victim and the rust covered Russian grenades urge me to find some reason for our actions. Using the spotlight on my rifle I make several sweeps of the area and have almost given up when I notice a tiny crack in the wall once hidden by the bed. Pulling out a brick reveals a hole that would be large enough for someone with tiny hands. I reach into the crevice with my pliers and fish out its contents. The boy's most private possessions lie before me and paint the portrait of a child's life lived during war.

The first thing that catches my eye is a beat up spaghetti cord, like the ones used on the original SINGAR radios during the initial invasion of Iraq and Afghanistan. I can't imagine what a sight it was for a boy watching the massive tanks and trucks roll by, a parade of smiling soldiers with the arrogance to wave and drape themselves in American flags. He would have been about five years old. Next to the cord and scattered all over the floor are pictures of American soldiers torn from the newspapers over the last eight years. This broken family is one of many we came to free and protect. I look at the feet sticking out from under the pile and picture the baby face that lies with me in the room.

I try to understand. We did our job, did it well and yet, here I am searching for anything to prove we were right and this child's death necessary. Looking one last time at the treasured images I brush my hand across the pictures and scatter them across the room. I accept there are no clues within the thirteen-year-old's possessions and the ancient grenades he wore were merely fan jewelry, a teenager's imitation of a warrior. We got bad intelligence, hit the wrong house and people died. The old man, whose photo I carry in my shoulder pocket, the bomb builder we were supposed to grab and snatch, has probably never entered this home.

Leaving the ghost behind, I walk into the front room where Marti is still screaming in the face of the woman. Drenched in tears she no longer waits for the translation and repeatedly shakes her head. "What do you want to do?" Marti asks completely breaking character.

"They know anything?" I ask on my way to check on Q and his crew.

"Man, they are saying they thought the boy was working for the local police and I believe them." Marti releases the woman and she collapses onto the floor.

"We're leaving," I tell him and take the last grenade, dropping the vest in the middle of the room. The man and woman gasp as their eyes follow the vest on its journey to the floor. I wave the boys out and the couple erupts in tears and suffering never taking their eyes from their son's prized possession. Helicopters become audible as they position for our escape and drown the grief behind me. Doubt is death in combat and regret has no place here.

Relief spreads among the men as the copters bounce low and we rush to exit. We did our jobs well and the dry hole that we find ourselves in is not our problem. I know we are lucky, bad information can destroy an entire platoon, and I relish the jokes and satire around me. Battle humor is not for the weak of heart and for a moment I forget what the woman and her husband will find in their son's room. My own laughter startles me as Fish imitates Trap's bluster over the radio. The sound is strange to me and erupts easily as we leave our devastation behind. It's a good feeling to be among these men, knowing they are alive and confident.

We are barely back on the birds when we are given another mission and find ourselves rushing to save Americans ill equipped to battle in this world. I watch as the mood shifts. Some try to hold on to the moment yelling taunts at Q as he juggles the boy's treasured ancient grenades, but others begin to lock down, protecting their souls for the next jump. I let weariness envelop my body, too exhausted to dig deep and ready myself for what is coming.

My demons wait quietly and as soon as I close my eyes I feel Red's warm pat and hear his words. "You done good boy." Mike's laughter and grin envelop me. I thought these long dead men were at my back, guardian angels, their words a comfort, but today they seem more like ghouls taunting me with their laughter and comments. I vaguely remember my excitement less than forty days ago when I started this deployment. My pride in my men and our mission vanished at some point, but I am not sure when or why. It's the pills, or lack of sleep or . . .

"Gotta pay your dues, buddy," Mike's voice pours from the agonized mouth of a dead teenager with two wounds in his chest.

I scream back at the phantom, "I fucking paid them!"

Marti is in my face, "Paid who? We're 30 minutes out, any words?"

Nodding in agreement, I sit up and try to stretch away the past few moments.

"They forget we're saving their asses, right?" Marti smiles softly.

"Right," I respond as if I understand. "Get on the radio and tell them we're dropping in hot and it's a rescue. Be ready for anything."

"You okay?" My look gives Marti his answer and he quickly gets on the radio.

Too soon we are on the ground again and head-first into the gunfight. I can see remnants of the National Guard we were sent to save surrounded by their dead. I wave for the survivors to follow and join the attack, but they don't budge. I understand not everyone in this war was trained to enjoy suicide and not all soldiers have the will to win or die. Running toward the enemy fighters, we move farther away from the safety of the courtyard where we descended down ropes just seconds before. We are not alone. The birds that brought us here still hover one hundred feet above raining down metal to cover our grand entrance.

Into the unknown my men take up positions along the corners of the block and begin to take back ground violently borrowed by our enemies. Q is across the street directing Jenkins to mow down a group of hostiles stranded in the middle of the road behind a burning car. I watch their bodies become gobs of mush as his MK-48 machine gun finds its target. Jenkins stops to reload the drum of his weapon and looks to make sure I saw his accomplishment. I call over the radio and praise him for his accuracy, but my words stumble on the vomit that tries to force its way out of my throat.

Enemy gunfire surges once again and my boys take cover trying to weather the storm, but I remain standing, calling the enemy to my direction. I feel blasts of air as bullets scream by my face and instantly understand Charlie's choice and Mike's final grin. This is freedom and the desire to end this, all of this, takes hold of me. I smile down at Marti as I dare my enemy to give the release I seek. My friend looks at me in disbelief, mouthing the word "no" over and over. I know I should feel remorse for his pain, but nothing matters anymore except my devouring need to escape. Strangely there isn't any fear and for a moment almost bliss.

I am far ahead of my men and surrender to the purpose of my enemy. Trap watching a satellite feed from the comfort of the control room screams caution over the radio, but I don't bother to acknowledge his orders. I am very near my objective and his repeated angry yells drive me ever closer to my need. Alone, with only the sound of my heart pounding I race forward. I see myself as in a spotlight, so near to my enemy I can smell their body odor and embrace their hatred as my reward. Suddenly, as quickly I welcomed it, escape eludes me. God is laughing and those I've killed watch in pleasure as my men follow my lead and surge forward. I curse the bad shots of my enemy.

They are out in the open now scurrying like rats and I know the fight will be over soon. The taste of freedom which was almost mine is instantly replaced with the stale bile of disappointment. In anger, I call on the boys to demonstrate our dominance and break any opposing will. The helicopters overhead join our display of power. I see men evaporate into smoke and bodies consumed by fire. I watch the dismemberment of human beings changing them into some abstract artistic stain painted on the concrete surface of the road. Those few that survive run in panic only to find death at the hands of my men who have blocked the street. I stand completely still and gasp for air as men die in various stages of agony all around me and still I live. It is over. There will be no escape for those who tried to take this American Base or for me.

My boss is calling me every name in the book. Eventually, his noise does invoke a response. Sliding my hand down my side, running my fingertips along my body armor, I find the radio and turn it off. I savor this new space, this quiet. The men wait in silence letting their own senses take over in the hope of another target, but there is no more gun fire, only the stars in the black sky silently watching and a slight breeze cooling my back.

"Boss," Q draws my attention back to earth. I see a man standing before me; his mouth hanging open gasping for air, his body covered in sweat while drops of blood run down his face. "What do you want us to do?" he asks softly almost as if he were passing a secret. Removing my glove and reaching over to him, I wipe the blood off his temple with my thumb and smile approvingly. Slightly nodding to my friend, he turns and takes the lead of the team issuing instructions for the boys to pair up and search the rest of the complex. Standing in the middle of the street completely out in the open I watch Q raise his rifle and the boys follow him off into the darkness. Gratitude swells for my friend. Taking a breath, I feel the weight of my weapon slung on my back. It feels heavy and out of place. Reaching up, I tug at the strap to find relief, but the night sky takes my attention.

"You OK?" Doc's voice startles me like a ghost. I hadn't realized I wasn't alone.

"Fine" I tell him as gunfire echoes in the distance. Without hesitation we begin a hasty walk toward the sound of the fight. I take the lead and we move into an alleyway to cut across the block. Training and instinct take over as we both ready our weapons. Moving deeper into the labyrinth, I see a silhouette dart across the path and behind a building. I motion for Doc to stay back while I peek around the corner. The silhouette jumps into the shadows and scurries away. Footsteps fade behind another structure and I rush full speed toward my visitor. I don't bother to wait for Doc, and round another bend expecting to be greeted with gunfire, but nothing. Turning down a moonlit path I finally find the elusive shadow.

A young child is leaning over an old man and both raise their hands in surrender. The boy is shivering and rambles in his language pointing at the man who lies next to him. The old man is cradling his stomach where blood pulses out of a large gunshot wound. They wait for me to react, but I'm curiously drawn to them and find myself walking forward and kneeling down beside them. I say nothing and take their rifles, empty the magazines, and throw their weapons over the wall out of anyone's reach. I lean into the wounded and feel his pulse. His hands are cold and covered with calluses from working the land his entire life. He balls up in agony as I softly push on his organs. I stop the examination not wanting to cause any more pain.

The old warrior whispers to the boy in a comforting tone. The softness in his voice begins to fade and his eyes gloss over signaling the end, but instead he fights the inevitable and smiles lifting his hand and running the backs of his fingers down the boy's wet face, savoring the last thing he will ever see. The child leans down in a tearful embrace of protest. I watch them both in silence. The boy's tears reflect the moonlight like diamonds and the old man's breathing slows with rhythms of an evening tide. I envy his dying and the peace he will soon find. The moment is broken by the sound of footsteps on the gravel pathway behind me. Alerted I take aim and push my trigger to the brink before I see the uniform and know it is Doc.

I call out to him. Doc is wiping his brow in relief until he spots the others and draws his weapon towards the boy. I have his forehead in my sight as the medic tries to decode the situation. Raising his weapon he looks to me for instruction. I nod him over to us. I can see the gears turning in his head. He scans our perimeter smelling out any traps and drops his weapon to assist the wounded. Just like I have seen him do a thousand times, he examines the body like the machine he believes it to be. I can see the extent of the damage under the illumination of a small mag-light held in Doc's mouth and know there is little hope. The medic's frantic pace soon slows and stops. "He's done for," Doc whispers regretfully. Sitting back, he continues to wrap the man's torso covering the gaping hole in clean white gauze.

The boy looks to me and I can only shake my head. He's been brave long enough and sobs erupt as he buries his head into me. His tears soak through my body armor and shirt. He suffers like all children, loud, and with uncontrollable anguish. The old man on the ground grunts and quietly chokes catching our attention. His soul escapes his body and leaves a shell staring blankly at the night sky. The boy's loss becomes my own and we embrace no longer strangers or enemies, but as a father would his son, a son I may never live to have.

"We got to get him out of here," Doc interrupts standing over us. We are in the middle of a hostile area, a battlefield, and I'm sure my medic is wondering where all this sudden compassion is coming from. I nod in agreement and ask the boy where to take the dead. He stands quickly wiping his face and moves down the path waving for us to follow. Doc grabs the feet while I grab the shoulders of the body walking backward. Even though he was a small man, the weight of the human torso is always an awkward thing. Struggling to keep up with the boy and avoid the knuckles of the dead from scraping the ground, we attempt to show some reverence to the old man. The child leads us to the outskirts of the base and without any idea of where we are going, continue without question or complaint. I move deeper into the enemy's hands attempting to grasp onto the insanity of what we are doing. Suddenly our guide stops and we lay the body gently on the ground. I follow the child into the shadows of a building and to the outside wall and there he reveals the enemy's secret.

They had burrowed underneath the outer structure. The hidden tunnel was the way they entered the base undetected and were close enough for the assault. This was a farmer's strategy and I think of the old man's callused hands. Doc snorts in approval at their cleverness and I agree with a smile, but everything shifts quickly as the boy speaks into the hole and a voice replies. We both grab weapons and assume a fighting stance. Only the child's panic and out stretched hands stop us. My weapon grows heavy as I see his fear, so heavy I can't support its weight. It falls from my hands and the sling whips it around my back as the boy crawls into the tunnel and disappears.

Doc looks to me for orders and I whisper to get back and cover the hole. I am in unknown territory. The boy reappears suddenly from the darkness and in silence grabs the shoulders of the slain attempting to drag the body into the hole. I watch him struggle with a dead man twice his size for only a moment before stepping in to help. More voices from the other side of the wall make themselves known. The only thing to do is keep my focus on the body and continue to help the boy. The enemy instructs the child and we continue to make progress in the tunnel, but all their encouragement stops when they see me with the body. I'm sure I'm about to be shot.

The white bandages that Doc used to cover the old man's wound are now brown and soaked in blood. The mouth of the dead hangs open, filled with dirt from his journey through the tunnel. One eye is closed and the other covered in mud along with his beard. The sight weighs on my soul. I don't care what happens to me and continue to push the old man further into the tunnel. Every inch of progress takes all my strength, but I want to get him home away from me and this place. When the hole becomes too small for the body and me to pass together, I realize I am at the end of my journey. A set of hands appears and takes over the labor. They pull and I push until they completely seize the load. Leaning back in the tunnel I watch as the man's body slides out the other side and vanishes into the dark opening. The last things to leave me are his bare feet dragging on the bottom of the tunnel and creating two little valleys in the loose dirt. It is a path laid out for me to follow without question or fear. I break from the darkness into the moonlight and make eye contact with five armed men not more than two feet from my face.

Huddled shoulder to shoulder around the body, they all turn to me and stare without emotion. Their eyes are glowing blue in the moonlight and I can see rings of sweat on the armpits of the U.S. Army fatigues they wear over their native clothing. Their attention is quickly drawn back to the body that lies in their midst. There is a strange beauty in their composition like old paintings I have seen of the apostles standing over Jesus. My revelation expands as I see the man on the ground for what he was and myself for what I am. Without fear I join the group of men who mourn the fallen warrior. My enemies and I, armed and dressed for war, stand over the dead and listen while the young boy presides over the funeral rights, delivering the prayer in a strong, clear voice. I watch the child walk away and the men lift the dead off the ground. They hold him softly and follow the innocent in silence. I stay just long enough to see them disappear. There are no farewells and no one looks back as I enter the tunnel. The moment is gone, but its mark will remain with me.

The look on Doc's face tells me he didn't expect to see me again. He stands with his weapon drawn frozen in disbelief. "Back to the courtyard" I tell him. We walk back in silence, my mind at peace with the vision of a tiny hand held in mine and my own hidden wounds bound tight for the moment. The fire fight in the distance is winding down and allows the sun to rise. The sky buries its stars as I remove my helmet and feel its weight off of my neck. It is a waking dream as I move through the dead and dying. How strange to be in this place of death and so suddenly filled with life. The sun breaks strong over the horizon and reveals a scene I have viewed many times. Bodies are lying everywhere and Doc already has his sleeves rolled up executing his craft.

Like bees, men are swarming to assist the wounded, moving quickly they dart from one flower to next. Two rows of bodies dominate the ground in front of me, one for the dead and the other for those who may survive. Without thinking I gravitate to the dead, kneel over the first body and take a moment to see the face before covering it. I wonder who waits for this young man. Will it be a grieving wife, father, or children who lay hands on a flag covered coffin without understanding? I think about the long journey still to come for all those who lie before me. Each one will travel thousands of miles and be touched by hundreds of hands, tears will cleanse and prayers be whispered before these bodies will rest forever. The sound of those suffering around me breaks through my thoughts and I focus on getting us out of here, all of us, the living and the dead.

CHAPTER FIFTEEN

It must be thirty or more missions in and I am looking down at a plate carelessly piled with lobster and steak. It must be Friday, "surf and turf day" for all the armed forces deployed to both Afghanistan and Iraq. The feast signifies another week down and I'm not sure how many there have been. We are deep into our second month, seven or eight weeks gone I think, but all seems to be mashed into one event as I sit with my team in the Bagram Airfield chow hall. I almost feel reborn after a five hour dreamless nap, thanks to Doc's pharmacy and a long hot shower. No one has put a folder on my desk in half a day allowing all of us a moment of hope. There is a simple pleasure in sitting down to dinner with my friends.

This is our only time together in the fragile space between missions without fear or consequences. It is a moment where we can pretend that we are free men. The end of the deployment is in our sights and some even calculate the number of days left in our trip. Every man laughs and speaks excitedly about the end of our deployment, but we all jump when a metal tray clangs to the floor in the kitchen. On the surface my men and I are surviving and performing our duty with honor and selflessness. On the surface we keep up our appearance for appearance sake. Laughing together we taunt the war just out of our reach, but I smell the fear buried underneath every word as it mixes with the odor of over cooked meat.

Suddenly, the room feels over-crowded and the noise of too many conversations, clattering trays, and scraping chairs is almost unbearable. I focus on a young Afghani busboy grabbing plates and throwing them in the trash to ground myself. The noise in the room and the conversations of my men evaporate and I see nothing but the ten year old and his hurried tempo. We have much in common, our long shifts, endless repetition, and our unfailing servitude. He is like a machine, wiping clean the surface, grabbing the half full plates carelessly shoved towards him while he moves down the rows of tables. I watch as he slows and crouches low to the table he is cleaning. I'm on the edge of my seat waiting for his next move.

The child scans the room for onlookers. His posture is like a cat ready to pounce and I sit patiently visualizing my bullets removing his head. My hand is on the pistol hidden beneath my un-tucked shirt and my thumb slides onto the safety. It is a moment in time like so many others where instincts take over. I'm sure he's about to make his move, but my pistol's weight is fighting to stay in its holster. Minute fractions of a second can save lives and I'm hesitating. Instantly, like the moves of a magician, the child steals a piece of meat off a plate and it disappears into his mouth. As fast as the first morsel vanishes the next is grabbed and shoved into his cheek. He chews the tough meat quickly as he continues down the row with head bowed. I laugh a little too loudly startled by my own tunnel vision. No one notices the gun in my hand as I shift it back to its home. It's time to get out of here.

The laughter of my men joins my own. Some are still shoving steak in their mouths and others hover over their cokes as if they were beers, waiting for the next punch line. No one mentions Fish or the empty chair screaming his absence. The death of our brother this trip is too recent and painful to touch.

We haven't retrained ourselves to fill his seat and it remains as a stark reality. His laughter and stories should be leading the table. No one could make me laugh as quickly as my buddy from Jersey. His thick accent and dark humor were in stark contrast to his manners. Unlike those around me, Fish always sat at the table upright and I can still see him cutting his food into small squares like his mother most likely had done for him most of his life.

"Whatcha starin at? If you're wondering these be manners my friend," he snarls at me from the empty chair.

We were on top of the objective we thought, but the choppers dropped us in the wrong place and as they cleared the shooting began. My men scattered for cover under direct fire. Once I could see the gunmen I began our assault and called the boys forward to cover my advance. Fish landed close to me and was seeking protection behind a little abandoned fruit stand.

"On me," I told him.

"You're kidding, right?" He screamed over the gunfire and lit a cigarette. "Come on, I just lit this thing and they're not going anywhere. Hey, two minutes?" After a quick review of my face he continued, "It's your suicide, baby, ready to die when you are."

For the first two rushing steps Fish was in front, and just as quickly as his lead vanished so did his life. We were shoulder to shoulder when an explosion of blood and matter sprayed over my face and weapon. We were out in the open and I was forced to leave him and move on. When I found cover, I looked back to survey the damage. Fish was chest down, hands at his side, his helmet and most of his head gone. My throat tightens with grief staring at the empty chair. "Don't cry for me Argentina, it's your ass you should be worrying about cocksucka," Fish chuckles over the noise in the chow hall.

Grissom, the newest guy added to the team, unknowingly slides into the empty seat to get closer to the jokes and stories. And just like that Fish is gone forever. I am laughing among the group at the table and Marti nods a silent welcome back. We spend the next thirty minutes trading stories and our thoughts about home. Plans are made for our first evening off in some fifty days and tomorrow we will be given medals and Fish a final farewell.

Leaving the chow hall, most scurry off to the Base Exchange for snacks, phone calls home, and cigarettes. "Sixteen Candles" is our chosen film for the night and one of the team's favorites. The cool air chills my neck as Q and I watch them skip away like little boys without a care in the world. "You don't want to call home?" I ask and we both laugh. Q is in the same predicament as me, no one to call and no one to love except our work and ourselves. I know some of the boys were packing up Fish's things and I wanted Q to make sure to take out the cigarettes and lighters. His wife didn't know he smoked. I have a call to make and head to the TOC and Q strolls back to the house.

I wait for the runner to transfer the call into an empty office where I sit. When the line clicks and begins to ring, I know enough time has passed and Rachael was informed. It is my time to check-in, but this is never easy. Her voice is strong thousands of miles away, and once again I am amazed at technology. I picture her picking up the phone, possibly interrupting another conversation, a television program, her tears of grief. "Hello."

"Hey lady, it's Joe," I respond softly and her tears quickly follow.

"I saw the unavailable number and thought it might be him," her voice is broken by her pain and I don't know what to say next. I stay on the phone overpowered with emotion and wait for her to work through her tears.

"How did it happen?" Rachael's voice demands and she is ready to hear the conclusion to her five year marriage. I stumble to find a foothold holding back my own tears. "What happened to my husband?" Her words are angry and stern, but I'm not sure how to handle the question. A shield of Army regulations steps in. I'm required to reveal nothing except the canned answer that her husband died defending his country in the global war on terrorism, but she deserves more, much more.

"We were dropped into a gunfight. Fish and I pushed into the front trying to get the enemy, I was right next to him when he got hit, I'm so sorry Rachael, so sorry." My words sound hollow and pointless.

"You know Fish was so excited that you chose him to join your team; he worked hard to get himself ready to meet your standards and I was happy for him. He was so nervous the first day he reported to you. I met you the next morning."

"I remember." I tell her and try to see Fish's face, but the memory seems so long ago. I see myself laughing with Fish at her kitchen table. She was giggling too I thought, or was there something else?

"He was so proud to be your friend, but my husband was not like you. He was a good man and I knew back then you would get him killed. I didn't want to believe it, but I knew." Her breaking voice tells me it is taking everything that she has to hold back, but she finally sobs out her final message, "I never want to see you or your men again, ever, do you understand?" The line is cut dead as she slams down the phone

I'm not sure how long I sit in the empty room, but by the time I reach the house the boys are in their favorite places. Most of them have moved their bunks to watch the movie from within their sleeping bags. I see Fish's possessions neatly boxed and stacked. Everyone is out of their clothes and into their sleeping attire. Our huge plasma screen glows blue as Grissom fumbles with the buttons on the

DVD player. A chorus of sarcasm erupts as he struggles and is pelted with snack wrappers and cups.
Everyone is talking about our last few missions and
joke about the close calls we'd had the night prior.
They speak to me with gratitude over their night off
even though I have nothing to do with it. Fish is not
mentioned and the film finally begins with cheers.
Most will not make it through the first ten minutes
before they are overcome with sleep. I yell at Grissom to turn up the sound. He will have to earn respect among this crowd.

Morning comes as a relief and with disgust. I
slept little. I am a man who loves traditions but fucking hates ceremonies. Two hours later I find myself
standing on a stage made of pallets facing some random group of strangers. The ceremony is not to hon-
or the dead or valiant, but is being used as a photo op
for a general. My men and I stand at attention waiting. I know as soon as the Army photographer is
gone the general and his entourage will also vanish
rushing to their next scheduled engagement. The rifle that serves as the memorial for Fish looks like it
may fall. I can't help but think it will probably not
photograph well in its leaning position.

I break ranks moving to the center of the platform and remove Fish's helmet that rests on the butt
stock of his weapon. I grab the rifle and oil leaves a
residue of black soot on my hands. His rifle was
cleaned, but I am not sure by whom. None of my
men would have left such a thick coat of gun oil; it
makes the rifle sluggish and unresponsive. I pull my
sleeve over my hand and wipe down my lost soldier's
weapon taking all the excess coating away. It's not as
shiny as before but now suits the man I once called a
friend. Done with the rifle I turn my attention to the
pair of boots that rest in front, they too have been
cleaned removing any sign of battle. Anger engulfs
me. Stabbing the rifle into the ground behind the
shiny boots, I fight the earth and my power over-
comes any resistance it offers. The dog tags hanging
from the trigger fall and I catch them before they hit
to the ground. I take a moment to rub the grit away
with my thumb. They forgot to clean these. I hang
the chain back around the trigger and watch as the
dog tags gently fall away from my hand. When I
place the helmet on the gun it bows low to the front,
not because of any reverence but forced by the night
goggle mount that fits onto the forehead area. A

fresh coat of paint drips down onto the boots that rest empty below. We were told to paint the helmet because scratches and damage don't photograph well. Stepping back, I inspect the tribute and return to my place at the front of the men, fragile as thin glass and close to shattering into tiny pieces.

Trap marches over to the general and offers a sharp salute, snapping his entire body rigid during the process. The general returns a lazy response. It is another reminder we are not here to pay respect to the man I got killed only hours ago. We are here for a general to feel like he is actually in charge. The photographer is in a great position and taking shots at will. It takes all my strength to keep from strangling her where she stands. My boss turns to face me and my men standing shoulder to shoulder. The crowd of thirty or so personnel ordered to be here are perfectly still, but their wandering eyes show their impatience with the ritual.

"Master Sergeant Cevera," my boss calls from the side of the stage still in the position of attention. Staring forward I do what is required of me during this ceremony and nothing more. Two of the crowd in the front row look at each other and half grin, very pleased with themselves. Having worked in the same vicinity for so long, it must be strange for them to hear my name and rank. I look at them cold and they lock away their smiles.

"Present Sergeant Major," I call back saddened by what is to come.

"Sergeant First Class Hays," my boss calls the next man in the line.

"Present Sergeant Major," Q responds immediately in his deep tone. The two soldiers in the front look even more pleased now, glancing at each other again. A rare treat for them I suppose. I look down at the shrine to my front and feel Fish's eyes watching me from the crowd. I know his body is on ice back in Doc's office waiting to make the trip to the States, but I still scan the group fighting reality.

"Sergeant First Class Manuel-Luna," Trap continues.

"Present Sergeant Major," Marti answers without emotion. Head locked forward at attention I notice the balanced helmet and it looks like it may fall, but I stop any instinct to fix the situation. The helmet and the weapon do not belong to Fish anymore. They never did. As soon as the ceremony is over I'll return them to the armory where they will be re-issued to the next man to fill his slot in this war.

I think about the old man and his soft touch to the face of the boy. What I saw when I looked my enemy in the eye was nothing more than the terror I see in myself. None of this belongs to any of us.

"Staff Sergeant Fisher," Trap calls to the waiting crowd. No longer able to stay completely still they sway like trees. Hearing Fisher's name creates nothing inside. It is the silence that follows which resonates his place among us.

"Staff Sergeant Lucas Fisher," my boss repeats, and silence answers once again. The General moves behind the podium. As he walks into place the young private snaps to life aiming her giant camera and zoom lens as she sits upon the front of the stage. The General snaps to attention and immediately the shutter on the camera clicks. The private leans back and takes a new angle and is able to get my men and Fish's rifle with the general in the back ground. The camera clicks three more times.

"Staff Sergeant Lucas Taylor Fisher," commands Trap and the rifle falls. The helmet crashes to the ground leaving a streak of paint on the wooden platform. The camera women shifts back to the front and crops the helmet and rifle out of the shot. He is gone and it doesn't matter.

"Lucas," calls my boss, the final step of the Roll Call. Silence and an empty spot in the line are all that remain of Fish.

Five rifles fire five times. We stop flinching after the first two. Taps plays. The general speaks and the paint dries. Roll Call is complete.

CHAPTER SIXTEEN

My men and I are on our way back from a long mission. The price we paid for a welcomed day off. Most of the boys sleep on their backs enjoying the crisp fading day. The call comes in, Trap's voice dry and calm, "Kilo Hotel one-two, this is one-one. We have a situation developing about 50 clicks south of you."

"One-one go ahead," I call back.

"A forward operating base manned by some Alabama National Guard unit is being overrun by what sound like Uzbek and Taliban fighters. They sure could use your help." Q has also heard Trap's radio transmission and I tell him to get everybody up and top off on ammo and water. "I'm having the coordinates sent to the pilots now; you should be there in twenty minutes," my boss continues. "I'm sending you the satellite feed now. Be on the lookout," and with that the radio goes dead. Reaching into my backpack I pull out my laptop and open the feed. The screen reveals what Hell on Earth must look like.

The main building of the base is burning with the back side completely backed up to a cliff leaving no room for retreat. Most of the friendly forces have gathered in a defensive perimeter to the front in a good sized walled square that from the images looks like it may have been a nice garden once. I point to the middle of the square and tell the helicopter's crew chief where I want us dropped in. He nods and disappears to the front of the bird to tell his pilots. All over the feed are pulsing strobes of friendlies that have been cut off and are surrounded and separated from the main element. I begin to count the clusters who need immediate assistance but stop because there are simply too many. Hopefully they can hold on until we make it to them. I turn the laptop to face my men for them to see what awaits us. "Holy Fuck" is the only response and it comes from Marti. The rest are silent.

"We will secure the square and move into the fight from there. Stay on me and we can get most of these guys out of there. If things start to go sour, we regroup in the square, understood?" I look to my men and they nod in agreement.

"Five minutes" the crew chief announces and adds, "Good luck."

At the back of the chopper I turn one last time to face my men, "Lock and load!" They simultaneously pull the charging handle of their weapons and get ready for the fight below. Turning back to face the rushing earth below, I put my hand on the rope ready to drop it and us into the fight. Q is to my right doing the same.

He looks to me and holds his fist out and I softly punch it. "See you on the other side," he says. My answer is a grin as the pilots push the throttle wide open. The turbo charged engines of the helicopter scream to life accelerating us ahead. Quickly in range, our radios come alive with the horror being transmitted from the fight beneath us.

Men are calling for help in tears to no answer. Others scream that they are out of ammunition and need back up. I hear a voice call out that he has been shot in the stomach and wants to be saved. Every cry for help is only drowned out by another. Every sob of surrender is matched by more. Panic is everywhere and mixed with the fear of eminent death. Moments from now those on the ground will hear our choppers coming and hopefully it will inspire a last push for survival. The helicopters begin their gun runs and buzzing cannons shower salvation to those below. My countrymen below call out and rejoice at our arrival.

"We have bombers inbound in three minutes. Get on the ground and get your choppers clear," Trap calls.

"Roger that," I answer. The birds hear that bombs are soon to be dropped and bank hard to get out of the way. I see the cliff that backs up to the main building and with another hard turn we are over the square. Time to go. I pull the pin and the ropes fall away. As always I am the first on the ground. My men spring into action and immediately the strength of the enemy is apparent. They come in coordinated waves at the entrance of the square and with each pulse of aggression gain inches into the perimeter. Q leads a charge toward the front gate, urging his element almost out of the courtyard. He is yelling at the guardsmen to get up and join him in the fight. He even grabs one man by the collar and drags him along, but the private curls his body as small as he can and begs to be left alone.

"You fucking cowards!" Q's roar is so loud that it causes a temporary halt in the gunshots as everyone freezes to decode his words. Almost to the gate, Q and his group huddle to the side and peek out into the space beyond the courtyard attempting to plan the next push forward.

"Q," I call over the radio. He stops his recon and retreats back to cover waiting for my instructions. "Patience, brother," I caution working my way towards him. He looks to me confused. Kneeling next to him I continue, "Our boys are more important, we all get to go home when this is over." Q's eyes fall to the ground for a moment and then he nods in agreement. The bombers arrive calling down for us to take cover, and I respond with the order to drop their munitions dangerously close to our positions. The pilots turn their noses in our direction as Marti and the boys run the perimeter of the square telling everyone to get down. A soft hiss is heard from above and grows in volume. My men turn their eyes toward the sky and for a moment the gunfire stops and the square is filled with a reverent silence.

Before the sound of the blast, the earth flexes under the punishment shoving me up and off the ground. The deep bass roaring is the sound of giant plates of rock that sleep beneath our feet awakening and being crushed by the bombardment. A shock wave like a tsunami turns me over onto my back exposing my face to the unleashed hell fire. Almost burned by the cloud of black that overtakes everything, the breath is knocked out of my body causing me to gasp the air thick with debris and I begin to choke. Before I get my bearings another wave of destruction not as close erupts. On my hands and knees struggling to breath, I hear most of my men under the same strain. The walls of the courtyard remain tall and a cocoon of dust and debris. The cloud slowly comes alive revealing the soldiers within. It's time to get back to work and finish this.

We fight for hours in the darkness battling over a few feet of earth. I hear the screams of dying men and pray that my boys are safe. We will not be broken. Exhausted and bruised, we are still a deadly fighting machine to be reckoned with and through the starless night the enemy feels our wrath. Pills ingested, we push ourselves past human limits before finally claiming the courtyard where we began. I feel the battle shifting as we neutralize the mortar positions raining misery down upon us. Our territory grows and we brutally claim the surrounding buildings.

A Marine artillery battery comes on station fifteen miles away and begins a barrage of the nearby ridge line. The enemy's surge of aggression finally slows as the ground shakes. Q calls for the Marines to fire closer and closer to our position until the artillery men refuse to target any nearer to us and the base. A-10 Warthogs arrive as the sun rises. Two of them circle overhead raining lead from their canons until they run out of ammunition. They shout out as they fly off into the horizon returning to base and thank us for calling them. The pleasure is ours and I know the battle is won.

For the first time at midmorning I can walk upright and have time to check on my boys who continue searching for targets as our enemy pulls back in defeat. My men are perched high on rooftops to cover against any advances. I feel the swell of satisfaction at a job well done. Most of the killing is now performed by the National Guard who has found a second wind of courage. Gangs of privates suddenly fearless and shirtless wander through the battlefield executing wounded enemy soldiers. I see a group of young men taunting an enemy fighter who had been somehow buried up to his waist in dirt from the bombs the night before. He is trapped in his half grave begging for help. Q and I watch as the privates kick dirt onto him with their boots and drown him in the sand laughing and taunting until nothing is left except two hands protruding from the ground clenched in panic. All around the seeds of atrocity are planted, and I call for Q's attention, "gather all these fucks and place them on the rooftops in a perimeter. This is their house and they can defend it. It's time for us to get out of here."

"Roger that boss," Q answers and runs off herding groups of men to the roofs to relieve my boys. Pushing the broadcast button on my radio, I call for the boys to gather soldiers to relieve them at their positions and return to the square for extraction. I can hear the uneasiness of my men as they view the abuses surrounding them. Meanwhile the base officers and top brass are absent, refusing to come out and take control of the situation in fear of a mutiny. I walk through scattered groups of survivors with my hand on my weapon still ready for anything. The men we saved are beginning to see us as outsiders that threaten to expose their dark secret. I continue moving to ensure the safety of my men from our brothers in arms and try to hide the disgust on my face. The more I see the more I know it is time for our escape.

We accomplished what we had come to do. Over the radios my boys confirm what the airborne assets have already told me. "They're gone man," Marti's voice is exhausted and relieved. I express my concerns to him and Q and also the importance of getting the boys busy on the wounded. I know the safer these guardsmen feel the more willing they are to push the boundaries of morality. Revenge is sometimes the only medication left to drown the grief for fallen friends. We have all been enticed by the need to slaughter. Slinging my rifle onto my back, I call to my men to gather at the Casualty Collection Point (CCP). I set up half to create a defensive perimeter around the courtyard and the rest to help Doc in treatment of the wounded.

The boys appear in pairs and I hover by the entrance until all are accounted for. I am overcome with relief realizing not one of us was lost. Many are wounded, but we are alive. Doc takes charge handling the more serious injuries and orders the boys to start making rows of wounded and dead to make sure they are not mixed together. He orders some of the National Guardsmen to get off their asses and help and they begrudgingly comply. Doc is in his element and I take a step back to get out of his way. It was a productive night. My magazines are empty and my rifle still hot to the touch. The familiar sogginess of sweat is all over my body and sounds of pain fill the air while Doc works frantically on the wounded. Leaning over a dead American, I pull his magazines from the body and refill my ammunition. He was able to fire two bullets before he died. Looking around at the crumbling buildings and the many dead, it seems like such a waste, but this is the nature of this place.

Back in the courtyard where we roped in ten hours earlier and inspecting the perimeter, I feel the morning breeze kicking up dust and welcome the sensual experience as it cuts across my face. Moving inward to the rows of bodies I walk among the dead. They are stacked two high and swaddled with baby blue tarps. The corners are held down with rocks, but still struggle against the wind to hide their gruesome cargo. There must be over a hundred bodies and still the ranks swell as more and more of the living and dead are dragged in from outside the courtyard. The neat symmetrical columns of suffering grow with a seemingly endless expansion. The rows of pain, similar to names in the newspaper, are the only testament to what happened here and the loss that America has incurred. The mission is a success.

My men killed or wounded more than 200 people and I lost no one, but my relief is stolen by the continued scattered gunshots outside of the walls. Everybody knows the enemy is gone and what remains is the brutality of my countrymen in full display. My distaste grows and I am tempted to call out the officers to take hold of their soldiers, but I refrain. Right and wrong are no longer part of our lives. We crave only survival. Honor codes during war are almost laughable even though at times they are the only things keeping us sane. Who knows what I would be doing right now if I had watched as my friends and buddies were slaughtered.

Walking through the columns of dead I eventually reach the wounded. An older black man lying in a pool of his blood smiles up at me and I kneel down next to him. He is drenched in sweat with his midsection completely covered in Doc's wrappings. From his pocket dangle three syringes notifying anyone who cares that he is full of morphine. Next to him rests a steel plate that was supposed to serve as his body armor, but failed. These National Guard units are so underfunded they were issued body armor that was manufactured just after the Vietnam War had ended. The plate resting next to him has two huge holes where bullets passed uninterrupted. He might as well have been naked during the fight. Looking at his smile I assume it is the morphine that is about to speak. He reaches his hand out to me and I grab it. "How are you feeling, do you need anything for the pain?" I ask and realize how stupid the question is as I look into his glazed eyes.

"Is Tomas around here? I know he was hurt pretty bad," the man speaks through shallow breaths in the soft, sweet notes of a Tennessee accent.

"I don't know Tomas, but I'm sure he's fine. Don't worry I have some of the best medics in the Army with me," I half smile as I look across the court yard. The man laboring to breathe turns his head but the effort is met with the resistance of pain causing his hand to clamp down on mine.

"How about James you seen him?" the injured struggles to stay alert.

I look over his uniform and notice his rank. He is a First Sergeant and one of the men in charge of this unit. "Sorry First Sergeant, I don't see him either," I answer trying to release his grip and stand, but he continues calling for his men.

"James! Tomas! You guys here?" and with every contraction of his diaphragm more blood pours out of him. A puddle begins to accumulate around his lower back. He will be gone soon so I surrender and stay with him until the end.

"You need to lie still and be quiet," I tell him as he battles to sit up.

"Right here First Sergeant, I'm coming," a young soldier calls out and limps over to his leader.

"You don't worry son," the sergeant gasps. "I know these men, they are the best and going to take care of us. We're going to be all right, you'll see, we going to be just fine." The wounded man's hand feels cold to the touch and his grip is starting to fade. His eyes look past me while a small twitch in his cheek sets in. The young man reverently looks up begging for me to save his sergeant, but remains silent as his leader looks hard at me. "I used to be stationed in Fort Bragg and I saw you guys around."

"What makes you think I'm from Fort Bragg?" I ask.

"Oh I know, I can always tell one of you guys, I could pick you out of a crowd, trying so hard to blend in." The sergeant should not be talking, but now the young man looks intrigued and examines me more closely. The wounded speaks softly to his soldier, "I'm proud of you boys,"

"Thanks First Sergeant," the young man responds with tears running down is face. I wonder if he would be so proud of his men if he knew what they were doing just outside this courtyard, but the man misreads the look on my face.

"You got to understand this was our first fight." he coughs the words. "My guys did great. We're not like you and yours. We had no choice. All of us are here cause we were told to be, but I'm still proud to serve, yes, I am."

"I'm sure you are," I tell him, but look away. The pool of blood has now gathered around the toe of my boot. I'm surprised by the man and admire his nobility. Most soldiers die rambling, sobbing, or begging for help, but this First Sergeant does neither, he is coherent and still worries about his men. I've only seen a few men die with their dignity intact. This is a good man and by the look of the young soldier at his side, is an honorable leader, but the war does not care about such things. Today he is only a casualty.

"You don't get down, you hear," the man turns to the soldier no more than a boy. "I'm happy to give my life for our country. No reason to be feeling sorry for yourself. Tell the guys that they did good, real good today and their First Sergeant is proud."

I want to do anything else but listen to this. "I know you guys." He says looking at me again. I expect him to start rambling like all the others, but his spirit fights a little longer. "I heard about all the hell you guys go through to get where you are. It don't seem worth it to me. I saw you guys around base back at Bragg, always alone, never friendly. You always seem sad to me." I picture myself walking around base testing his theory and wondering if our isolation was self-inflicted. "How many fire fights you been in?" He manages another clench of his hand in mine. "How many?" he presses.

"A couple," I answer with a soft smile.

The man's eyes focus on me. "What's your name?" his eyes are as sharp as an eagle. "Joseph." It feels strange to say my name out loud.

"I feel sorry for you Joseph. Men shouldn't have to be the way you are." He smiles, relaxes his face and the Sergeant is gone from this world. I gently place his hand on his torso within his other hand and remove my glove. For a moment I cradle his cheek and feel the truth of his words. I try to remember a time in my life before the war started, but can't seem to gain a foothold in my memory. The choppers' growing rumble calls me back into the present as I slide my hand down the sergeant's forehead and close a good man's eyes forever.

CHAPTER SEVENTEEN

"Get it done and make it fast," a phrase my boss loves to use and uses often. The manila folder slides across the desk and into my lap because it takes a little longer than normal for me to close my hands. My reflexes are dull and nonexistent due to a lack of sleep and the amphetamines I have been taking, both needed desperately to keep going. I can only stare at my hands. Like the rest of me, they are bruised, beaten, and just plain out of gas. Everything is sore and hung over from the past few months of this deployment. There has been no break or rest for me and my men and even though I'm in no shape to do anything but shuffle back to my bunk and sleep for days, I am being told once again to go out and hunt because there is a job that needs to be done and that supersedes all else.

"Don't think I don't know what is going on with you," the voice of my boss is like a fork on a chalk board. I have led my men beyond the edge of the earth and destroyed countless lives on both sides, but for the moment I panic and wait for something to come out of his mouth that might incriminate my behavior. Staring at his chapped lips I expect Trap to verbalize all the doubts and depression that swarm my thoughts. Gradually the weight of my head pulls at the base of my neck. Despite my best efforts to focus, I am losing the battle to stay awake. My boss and his pointless words begin to fade out and the past few months' whirlwind heat of destruction slides blissfully away. I balance in a space between the conscious and unconscious and struggle to stay awake long enough to find out what will happen next. I wait for my boss to talk himself out. I wait for the dread that plagues every aspect of my being to be quenched with another mission.

A stack of stapled papers smack me in the face and I wake up. "Jesus, take your pills already and make it a double." Startled, I look up at my boss and realize I am low in my chair barely clinging to the armrests. I'm not sure how long I was asleep, but Trap is yelling at the top of his lungs. He screams a tirade of all my mistakes during my past more than a hundred missions and makes sure that everyone in the nearby control room can hear. He continues to work himself out of breath while I sit in a daze. Earlier, I couldn't find the dexterity to tie my boots.

I am a methamphetamine addict on a binge, losing total track of time, and prone to fading off for moments. My boss knows he is pushing me and my men far beyond what is right, but it doesn't seem to matter. I need to get to work, but find myself staring at the little paper strips blowing on the air-conditioning duct. Trap is digging through his files, "hold on a second I got something else for you." I don't respond and zone out on the pattern of the carpet fibers moving like waves underneath my feet. It is becoming even harder to stay conscious as my mind works to grasp some footing among the fog of exhaustion. My eyes are open and I'm still sitting in my boss' office, but no one's at home.

Trap, the king of small talk, is rambling on about some young hot girl that works at the coffee shop on the strip. He is amazed how she spends her evenings and days off giving hand jobs for twenty dollars to all the other soldiers stranded in this combat zone. Trap's voice fades into the background. I know exactly who he is talking about and her face appears swirling in the fibers of the carpet. I see her smile at me, begging me to give her twenty bucks so I can take my turn, but our moment is interrupted by Trap laughing loudly as he describes the length of the line outside her living quarters.

Never saying a word and barely acknowledging his presence in the room infuriates my boss and he yells even louder, promising to pull me off my team and make me a coffee runner. I look up expressionless at his threat; he is crossing a line and sits back down lowering his voice and smiling, knowing he now has my attention. Trap tells me no one cares about my performance or my men and that the brass is impatient with the lack of results of our campaign. As if the bad intelligence is somehow my fault, he warns me that my men are going to be sent out over and over again until we make a newsworthy high priority catch. He promises we will not sleep until we deliver and spells out the hell to come if we don't cough up something big. He talks of the men I will lose and vomit rises in the back of my throat.

I say nothing in response to his words and sit low in my chair thinking about the loaded 9mm pistol that is tucked under my shirt. Trap is pleased with his performance. Over the years he has asked me for the impossible and I always delivered. He is the man who co-opted me into this life because he claimed to see my potential. Trap promoted me and put me in charge of the team he once ran and welcomed me into his home and adored me like a son. He was never asked to do what he now demands of me. All of this pressure because America is not decisively winning the war. I suppose they want heroes and ticker tape parades, but we are not heroes and when I entered the special operations side of the house, I never expected or wanted to be recognized.

Sitting in Trap's office the thought of a parade makes me chuckle. I look at my boss and his disgust. This is a man who would stop at nothing to protect his vanity. I know he was reprimanded by the powers that be and my men will pay for his embarrassment. Rising, I understand what he is willing to sacrifice to maintain the good graces of the brass. I'm not sure why I laugh opening the door, but Trap snorts signaling another round of shouting. I need to leave and break the news to the boys that we are going out again, but can't help rolling my eyes as one last fuck you to my boss.

He erupts in shock at my insubordination, but his words are meaningless. I have already endangered my team enough by my actions so I turn back to face him and force an expression of general interest in an effort to repair the damage. Trap sits and tells me a story about himself years ago. He explains how he almost threw away his career because he was growing impatient with the Army's promotion policy. I am thinking about the folder in my hand and what the night holds for me and my men. Attempting to keep my eyes and face pointed in his direction my mind begins to fade away once again.

Trap laughs, but I miss the joke. I smile in fake attention as my boss leads his monologue back onto himself and his greatness only to emphasize how I'm not fulfilling his expectations of me. He concludes with the fact that there are other teams that are getting more recognition than mine, but we both understand that is not true. I know the other teams are struggling and the hell they are experiencing is similar to our own. Sensing that I am not paying any sort of attention, Trap fights the urge to start another screaming fit and orders me to leave. I exit his office in silence.

In the TOC, I see Q looking as tired as I feel and waiting at the other end of the aisle. I think of Marti earlier attempting to button his shirt again and again without success. We are malfunctioning, damaged and beyond exhausted. Still my boss pushes and shoves, and is careless with our lives as if we are nothing. Q knows the routine and reads the signs that something is going on. He also notices the folder in my hand and cannot hide his look of despair. As I walk towards him, we are interrupted by two quick whistles, the second one higher in pitch than the first. It is the same sound Trap uses to call his beagles back home. The whistle sends a piercing pain through my throbbing head and causes me to jump from the star-tling noise. I see Trap waiving me back to his office. It is his way of showing everyone in the room who is in charge and reestablish the pecking order.

All eyes are on us after hearing the screaming monologue earlier, and I can tell by his grin that my boss is pleased with his display of power. He yells across the room for me to "hurry up," the same way he would call a cherry private, choosing again to dis-play his dominance over me. It is the price I pay for my lack of enthusiasm about our next mission. Even though I haven't said a word of protest or pleaded our exhaustion, Trap, my one man jury, might as well be judging me for treason. I walk towards him without changing my pace, expressionless, but I feel my anger expanding.

I don't stop until I am less than an inch from his body, halting just short of a collision. Forcing all the air out of my lungs through my nose, I release my hot breath on the top of his head and see the little hairs move around his bald spot disrupted by my exhale. Trap instinctively steps back looking confused. I don't budge, standing tall and using my height advantage to scowl down at him. His expression changes to rage as he senses others watching and my exhaustion falls away at the sight of his ego. I feel the barrel of my pistol and wait for some arrogant comment to come from his scowling mouth, but nothing. Give me a reason. The man who struts around the office like an outlaw without a care in the world has nothing to offer me. Trap looks nervous.

Silent, I hover a little longer to make him regret his decision to fuck with me and ensure that he will stay out of my way for the rest of the deployment. I hold his gaze and slide my hand into my pocket.

Trap's eyes follow my every move. His mouth hangs open as he prepares himself for whatever surfaces. He looks scared and I savor the sight. A sigh of relief swells over him as two small white pills emerge and make their way into my mouth. My next round of amphetamines collides with the urge to vomit as they begin their journey into my psyche. I turn and leave without ever having to say a word; sure that I have jeopardized everything I have ever worked for in my career. I leave Trap knowing that he will find a way to spin this to his advantage.

Back into the noise of the command room Q still waits for instruction at the other end of the chaos. I signal for him to gather the men and walk deeper into the TOC. My thoughts do not dwell on the flushing sound that now accompanies my career, only on the task ahead and how it needs to be completed in order to get as many of my men out of this hellhole as possible. I think about the days when I stood in awe over the things I felt Trap could accomplish on and off the battlefield, but now with this sinking feeling in my chest I have nothing but resentment for the power he has over us. The glory days are over; we are nothing more than pawns scrambling blind in search of a prize that will justify our existence. The pills are taking hold of me.

The familiar flutter in my stomach begins to grow accompanied by a slight twitch in my hands. I franticly gather my papers knowing I will soon not be able to sit still long enough to hold a pen or a thought in my head. Sweat rolls down my back and I begin to panic and drop the mission folder. I have to get to my men before the speed takes over and I can no longer brief the mission or put my gear on. The man sitting next to me senses my terror and attempts to help me gather the mess. I stop him by pulling all the papers and maps to me, cradling them close to my chest like a baby. My hands are trembling and I am engulfed with a desperate need to get away from the crowd and noise that rages inside these walls.

At that very moment Trap emerges from his office. Light on his feet and almost gleeful, he walks to the end of my row looking straight at me. He is holding another folder in his hand and I freeze watching him as more sweat rolls off my chin and my state worsens. My boss yells for a runner, who takes the folder from him and moves quickly, carelessly tossing it onto the piles of paper covering my desk. I haven't looked at the mission I was given in his office and with this new folder, I can't help but see myself as a rogue pit bull being put down for biting his owner. I keep a cold watch on Trap chatting with a young female private at the coffee maker. Their laughter irritates as I turn back to my desk. While I hunt tonight he will sleep.

Any combat experience that the brass may have had was during Desert Storm and it lasted only a matter of weeks. No General or decision maker has ever had to endure what my men have and none of them know the strain of manning the same life or death post every day for years. Bitterly, I think about all my deployments, all of them violent and bloody, and the broken men and souls left as our legacy.

I stare at the two folders on my desk knowing I have handed my boys a death sentence. In this kind of state, if you blink too hard a tear may flow and this is not a place to show weakness. The folders call for me, but I simply can't muster the strength to oblige. I scan the room. Men and women are all moving around me with purpose and urgency. They should feel the pride of a day's work done, but the day never ends and what was done? I am soaked in sweat and my emotions ebb and flow leaving a wake of scar tissue. The folders rest as if tombstones marking the end of someone, marking the end of me. I grab a cigarette and hold it tight between my lips. I'm tired, scared, and cannot find the courage to look inside and see what awaits me. I want to go home.

The folders are in my sweating hands now and I leave the ghosts of my fingerprints on their covers. The War is a ravenous animal. The men, like my boss who are in charge, think they can sway its favor by offering an endless feast. It doesn't matter on whom it feeds, but only on an endless supply of fresh meat. Looking down into my lap, I feel the war's hunger swelling. Saliva dripping from its blood stained fangs, the click of its talons as it stalks ever closer. Whatever lies inside these folders can only add to the nightmares I work so hard to suppress. I know what once gave me solace cannot save me now.

My mind is moving fast, jumping from image to thought at the speed of sound. I see my men falling on the battlefield and their suffering. I see the change in them brought on by the War and watch as it consumes them; and I wonder if they will ever be able to manage anything else. I stand among them and understand what I was and what I have become. I am defeated, but not by my enemy. Like a good soldier I played my part. I plunged into glory without question, without hesitation, always ready to lay down my life for my country. A thousand miles marched and only casualties and sorrow fill my boot prints. This is not a place for honor, glory and country. The game has changed. My heart is not enough, my soul not enough, and my life will not be enough.

My heart races and hands shake as I slam the folders onto the desk. I know I can stop this and save the lives of my men. Trap's door is open. He and this place can go fuck themselves. I have given everything. I feel my pistol, waiting and patient. There is only one way to stop this insanity and it will end here today. I hear Trap's laughter as I walk straight and proud to his office. The drugs are pulsing through my brain and I imagine his look of surprise as I end him. We are simple machines, trained to kill and be killed without complaint, but even machines can be pushed too far, beyond their breaking point. It has been a long time since I was unafraid and completely sure.

CHAPTER EIGHTEEN

Before I can reach Trap's door, men begin to yell across the TOC at each other. I pause with my hand on the pistol that promises relief and feel the rhythm of the room rise. I hear the drum rolls and horns of triumphant music as the screen lights up and doves fly from the Koran. I hold my breath waiting to see Americans being killed and bodies stripped. My hands close into fists. The screen suddenly goes black and the room fills with silence as my rage swells. All tense, anticipating the next transmission to appear. The screens quickly glitch and bloody swollen lips, cracked from dehydration and clinging to dried blood fill the wall. The camera pans back to see the entire face of a blindfolded, young woman and then four more victims appear, panting in fear with their eyes covered. Old habits die hard and I move towards the screen as if hypnotized. Killing my boss will have to wait.

Five people in western clothes are revealed on their knees with hands behind their backs. Their faces show the abuse of their captivity. Six men with their identities covered with baklavas hang over their hostages pointing AK-47s. One of the masked men takes center stage and begins to speak. Holding in his hand the press credentials of the captives he scrolls through each reading their names. I don't understand what is being said, but an interpreter stands off to my right and begins to translate. I barely hear the translation; his voice cannot compete with the hostages shivering in terror.

"Tell my wife and kids I love them!" a young man at the end of the row cries out interrupting the ravings of the kidnapper. Another masked man comes from off camera and strikes the captive in the back of his head with the butt of a rifle. He slams face first into the ground as the other hostages break composure wailing and screaming. The broadcast goes dead. The command room explodes into a rush of panic. A runner sprints past me into Trap's office and I follow. No one notices the gun in my hand and I slip it back underneath my shirt. My boss stands behind his desk holding a folder.

"Terps say the reporters are going to be beheaded at Noon. The source of the broadcast was close. If you leave now you can make it," Trap speaks without apology. I can hear them replaying the broadcast back in the main room. My mind is frozen on the man calling to his wife and I wonder if his children will ever see him again. I take the folder and open it. Someone had already taken screen shots of the broadcast and printed the faces of the hostages. Looking at the five pictures, I know what needs to be done.

"Send the grid coordinates to the chopper pilots, I'll call you when we are airborne," I state and leave Trap's office as the speed continues its rush. Two men are waiting just outside, both of them holding papers.

The first one begins his brief, "This is the satellite imagery of the compound that sent out the signal. It has been on our *Intel* list for some time so luckily I can send you with good photos of the target building. I've already highlighted the areas where the hostages most likely are being held." I glance at the packet and stuff it into my folder.

The next young man takes a deep breath and speaks rapidly, "I made copies for you and your two team leaders. These are photos of the area surrounding the target building; to the west right here," he points his finger at the image. "This is the town square. A crowd is gathering there right now so expect to have to deal with that and it is also where the beheading will take place." I take his gift.

"Thanks," I offer and head to my desk. There I begin the familiar routine of taking off my dog tags and putting the I.D. card into my drawer.

"Master Sergeant Cevera," a voice calls from across the room. I look up to see who it is. Everyone's frozen and looking at me. My eyes find the familiar face who called out and recognize the Navy SEAL who fought with me during the horror of Tukar Ghar. He alone understands what awaits me and my men. For a moment our eyes hold, "Good Luck Sergeant." I can only wink at my brother in reply. Q is already at the exit hallway geared up and holding my vest, helmet, and weapon. Putting on the vest and slinging the M-4 over my back, I hear my boss call out of his office.

"At Ease!" The whole room snaps to a standing position interlocking their hands behind their backs. I look at Trap who is at the position of Parade Rest, eyes locked onto me. I inspect the room one last time, my boss salutes. I snap to attention and salute him back. Out of respect he waits for me to lower my hand first and I nod in acceptance.

"Carry On!" I shout and am out the door.

The sun is still waking in the east; the morning gusts have faded and left behind their cooling presence. Walking with Q, I show him the photos in the folder and brief my rough version of the plan. I can hear the helicopters spinning up in the distance making Q and I instinctively walk faster. A glance at my watch, tells me it's going to be tight but we can still make it. Q runs ahead and bangs on the changing room door, "It's time to go boys." I don't stop and continue along the path to the helipad praying the speed shake will subside. Soon the sound of gravel under my feet is swallowed by my boys as they file out of the door in single file. I don't say a word or look back until stopping before the two choppers that will take us to our battle. I inspect and offer a half smile of approval to each of them and stick out my fist. Each man pounds it as they pass. They are ready and for the moment, so am I.

Q calls to tell me he and his element are a go and Marti nods in agreement. A look to the crew chief and the birds lift off without hesitation in a roar at full throttle. "X Ray 21 this is 25, we are on our way," I signal to my boss.

"Roger that 25" is the quick response. The crew chief is breaking open more ammo boxes to make them easily accessible during the mission. The 20mm canon is test fired once we make it out of the airfield. I see the ground rushing below and the familiarity brings a small sense of comfort, but we are night creatures, stealing in and hidden in the darkness. Daylight is not our friend.

I turn on my radio and switch to **Broadcast All**. "Listen up, as you know we are very short on time, so I'll make this simple. We stay together and get the fuck in and get the fuck out." I pause for a second to pull myself together and to sound strong on the radio. I'm not sure how much we have left to give and turn back to the men. Each of them is going through their pre-mission routine; they look fierce and determined, but also exhausted, beaten. The edginess is gone, the saggy eyes and dirty faces are calm and lethal, but is it enough? I speak to Doc and call for another dose. He refuses. I know the risk. A man's heart can explode. I have seen them collapse in spasms when pushed to these extremes of drugs and fatigue. I press and my medic reluctantly responds. I radio Q to do the same and broadcast again, "These people need our help, their families need our help, let's do this right and get them the fuck home."

"X Ray 25, this is 21, over" the radio blares.

"21 this is 25 go ahead" I respond.

"Looks like we have movement on the target; they are relocating the hostages to the square, over."

"Roger that 21, hostages on the move."

"25, I'll keep you posted when they're out in the open, 21 out," my boss has become our eyes.

Calling to the chopper pilots I change the plan accordingly. I know when the enemy hears the noise of our approach they'll retreat into the target building. Dragging five blindfolded, terrified hostages two blocks back to their compound will take time. If we can cut them off from retreat and trap them on a side street away from the town square, we may just be able to buy enough time in the confusion to get the journalists out. I transmit over the radio the new plan and change in the drop zone. Pilots inform me they are burning too much fuel at this speed and need to slow down or they will have to return to base and refuel. I call back to my boss and ask for two more choppers so we won't be stranded. He responds to my request, "I'm on it," slamming down his head set and rushing to find our second pair of Chinooks.

"Five minutes," the crew chief announces.

"Lock and load!" I call to my men and pull the charging handle on my weapon. The action feels smooth and correct, my breath suddenly slow and deliberate. My boys stand and line up behind me ready for the fight and I can feel the surge of their dose. I'm at the back of the chopper hand on the ropes that will take us into battle.

"I got eyes on the captives!" my boss calls out excitedly, "They are moving them now, looks like five people with bags on their heads and about twenty hostiles."

"Roger that. Let me know when they make it to the square." The timing's good and it feels right.

"Listen up," I call out, "We cannot let them make it back to the target building and give them time to execute the hostages. Marti, you and your boys have crowd control. Q you're with me. Good clean shots boys." The men are excited now. They yell and howl as the hunt is about to begin. There is no ambiguity here, not today.

"One minute!" the crew chief calls out. I step closer to the end of the ramp looking out over the city below. The pilots are rushing us in faster and harder than I have ever experienced. I prepare for the G force as this bird flares to a complete stop hovering over the objective. Grabbing the ropes that will soon fall, I take a deep breath and hold.

Nerves and excitement overtake my boss as he screams into the radio, "Hostages are in the square, but they hear you coming, wait, wait! They are pushing back to the target building. I repeat they are pushing back to the target building. Get in there Joe!"

The chopper pilots hear my boss' last transmission, and rev the birds even harder. Lower to the ground we ride, the choppers whining under the strain. At this rate they may be burning more fuel than will allow them to get back, but it seems the price they are willing to pay. "Ten seconds" the crew chief screams. The 240 machine gun mounted on our bird comes to life. I can see Q's bird in trail also beginning its gun run. The chopper banks hard to the left almost turning completely around. My legs lock as I try to stay on my feet fighting the force pulling me down.

Reaching to my radio with a free hand, "Boys, I'm out the door." The burn on my hands focuses me as I try to maintain my grip on the rope, pull the pin and let it fall free. It's my turn. I take a last step off the back ramp and begin my descent. The dust hides our arrival and I spot Q beginning his drop less than fifty feet to our south. The choppers rain lead and steel to cover our entrance and have done their job well today. On the ground I step forward and take a knee waiting for the rest of my team to arrive. To my left I see a masked enemy holding an AK-47 taking aim at Q and his men. I raise my weapon, completely sure of myself for the first time in months, and put two rounds in his head. Q hears the sound of my rifle and sees the result of my work. I get a rare smile and nod, but note more armed men working toward our position. It's time to go.

"25 this is 21, move south then hang left at the end of the block, that will put you next to the target building. The hostages will be heading right towards you."

"Roger that, I'm on the move," I call back to my boss. Standing now, I turn back to my boys who are now following in a V formation and ready to move into the fight.

Marti looks to me, "Lead the way, boss."

We start our movements toward the hostages away from the drop zone and our protective brown out. The gun fire begins to heat up. Q and his men are on both sides of the street facing a small group of five armed men. My grenadier Thompson and his stocky frame loads a round on the move and fires placing his 20 millimeter grenade in the center of the hostile group never breaking a stride. They only have enough time to realize he has killed them before the explosion turns them all to mist. Almost to the corner we make a left turn as gunfire erupts to our rear. Marti directs his men to cover our advance. I peek back just in time to see him hunched behind a parked car. He takes aim and squeezes three times. Three head shots are the result. I can't help but feel pride. The rest of the hostiles seeing the heads removed from their comrades scatter in panic.

I call my men to push forward and without hesitation I find myself at the corner and onto the street where the hostages are coming. "25 this is 21, you are right on track, captives are about 400 meters to your front heading right for you. The target building is the second building on your right. I don't see much activity there. Also 25, be advised the choppers can only be on station for another 10 minutes. They are out of fuel." Trap is keeping us informed. I set the timer on my watch for seven minutes and move into the street. My men fan out into two columns skirting the sides.

Three steps in and gunfire erupts. The boys scatter searching for life saving cover and I dive behind a column that supports the outer wall of the target building trying to make myself as small as possible. I wait out the wave of fire. There is a pause as our enemy stops to investigate the damage they hope to have caused us and we strike. "Now!" I call to my men. Like the waking dead, my men stand and begin our assault forward. I take the middle of the street and find Q at one side with Marti on the other walking with determined focus. Our guns are raised, each of us finding our targets with cold precision. The body count begins to rise. As we pass the target building a hand full of enemy guards file out to stop our advance. They don't have a chance and their bodies dance as a wall of 5.56 rounds find their home.

A quick magazine change and glance at my watch tells me we are running out of time. I pick up my pace. Q and Marti stay with me. 100 meters further and I can see the hostages down the block. They walk hunched over, heads covered with burlap, stumbling with the pushes and pulls of their captors. I find a target and instruct my men to focus their fire on the hostile closest to the hostages. I tell them we have come too far to take the journalists home in body bags. They hear my call and answer in a wave of focused energy. My men and I are on the attack and everywhere I turn armed fighters are falling. I can feel the air move as my boys put their rounds inches from my head. It feels safe and warm.

Closer now, I hear the sobbing terror of the reporters, who have no idea what's happening. I want to call to them and let them know it's going to be okay, but there is still too much work to be done. I'm running out of time. My enemy feels their victory slipping away and falls back to the town square. I can see each hostage being dragged back by an armed escort. "They are making a run for it!" Marti shouts. A moment of panic sets in; if we take too long the choppers will have to leave and refuel abandoning us to our fate. We are outnumbered in a hostile area and despite our training and abilities we won't last the night. This is it, the tipping point, if I fail now my decision will cost each man under my command his life.

An instant of calm sets in. A deep breath passes through my lungs and I look back at the two elements of my team. Q is standing in the middle of his group pointing toward the hostages. I can't turn my head fast enough to see the spray of blood and brain matter jetting from our enemies' bodies. They begin to fall. One of the armed escorts loses his grip on a hooded prize while his face contorts in the agony of the kill. The hostage falls to his side and begins to struggle to get up. The next captive breaks free and starts to run blindly toward us. I can feel the collective bodies of my men tense up as they try to cover his desperate scramble. I am on my feet running toward the bound man as he struggles to gain his balance. "Get down! Get down," I scream at the hostage as I rush towards him.

Behind him the masked enemy raise their weapons and focus on their prize. I also take aim trying to save the journalist, but his body blocks my shot. I lunge forward slinging my rifle to my back and place my life in the hands of my boys. I can hear the air rush out of the man's mouth as I collide into him. Falling to the ground and wrapping my arms around him, I turn us both so that my back faces the enemy. Releasing all the air from my lungs, I wait for the strike of bullets to assault my body armor, but none come.

I roll onto my back and draw my pistol and begin to fire. Looking over the captive's head, I see my men wide eyed, mouths open, screaming, charging. Their roar overtakes the sound of all the shooting, fire burning in their eyes, each one leaving a shining trail of bullet casings ejected from their rifles.

I turn to face the other hooded captives screaming, "Get down, Get down!" All of them manage to fall to their knees. With the hostages out of the way it only takes a few more seconds to clear the rest of the street of any danger. It is done.

The journalists are now in the arms of my men and I slowly remove the hood from the man who lies next to me and cut the zip ties that bind his hands. He rolls away from me still terrified for his life. A moment later he realizes I am not his enemy and smiles in relief. "Can you walk?" I ask.

"I can run, if you need me to," the freed man answers quickly. Under four minutes remain for the birds.

"We got to go boys. Now!" I call my men back, "Choppers are running out of gas and this town is about to be all over us." Handing my hostage off to Marti, Q and his element begin to push back the way we came. I hear the helicopters moving closer to pull us out as we turn towards the drop zone. All my men are accounted for. I lost no one during the fight. Jenkins is injured and Grissom bleeding, but all will survive and my emotions swell in relief.

"Wait, wait!" a battered woman stops us. "Phil is still in the truck. They put him in there when they took us out of the house." A low sadness falls over me as I scan the group and count only four hostages. My mind races to find a solution. The helicopters have landed and lowered their ramps for us to board. The crew chief is waving us in wildly.

"Where is he?" I ask.

"There's a white truck with a camper right as you enter the square. He was in the back last time I saw him," the journalist pants heavily.

Two minutes remain. "I'll go get him."

Q freezes in his tracks, but is unsurprised by my answer. "And I'll go with you." My men stop in disbelief.

"No. Get on the birds and stay as long as the choppers will let you, if I don't make it back get the fuck out of here." Q shakes his head no. "That is an order," I state in the sternest voice I can deliver. "Well, go on, I'll see you in a minute," I address all my men and they slowly move toward our rides. I can feel Q's eyes burning into the back of my head, but sprint to the square and don't return his gaze. I run as hard as I can. No time to feel the burn in my legs or the adrenaline falling away. One thought, get the last hostage, simply one foot in front of the other and don't think about the scream in your lungs. Run. Past the target building and only 50 meters from the square I hear yelling ahead.

I slow my pace and raise my weapon in preparation for the upcoming fight. Stepping softly I come to the entrance of the square and see six armed men hovering over their last captive. They are taking turns kicking his ragged body, scolding him as punishment for our intrusion. The victim manages a soft moan and winces after each blow and curls himself tight for protection. The largest of the enemy yanks off the hood of the hostage and pulls a machete from his belt and laughs. The other five step back to distance themselves from the blood that will splatter from the beheading. Rearing his blade high into the sky with both hands clasped tight around the handle, the executioner mutters something in *Pashto*, while the hostage clinches his eyes and holds back his sobs.

I pull my weapon tight into the shoulder knowing I only get one shot at this. Exhaling through my nose I pull the trigger. My M-4, which had always been one of my best friends, has never failed me and neither has my aim. I pray to any god that will listen to not let either desert me today. The first round strikes the enemy holding the machete and blows the jaw off of his face. Dropping the blade to cover his wound, he loses a hand as my second round shoots through the roof of his mouth and out the back of his head. The man next to him goes out without a fight and hasn't time to process what is happening as a bullet to the base of his skull turns him off like a light. Two of the enemy see me now and raise their weapons. I get one before he has time to pull his trigger with a double tap to the chest. With the next I'm not so lucky. His bullets are skipping off the ground just to my right and I dive to the left still shooting. One of my rounds grazes his shoulder sending him in a turn. A perfectly timed shot meets his face as he spins to the ground going limp along the way. I fire more rounds down range as I continue the charge. A quick magazine change and I keep on with my drive. The rest scatter like rats returning sloppy fire as they retreat.

I'm to the last hostage now. He has a look of shock on his face as he tries to gain hold of the last few seconds. I cut off his restraints and ask, "Phil, can you walk?"

"I think so," he whispers.

"Good because we have to go," pulling my pistol from my belt and handing it to him, "do you know how to use this?"

"Yes," his eyes fix on the 40 caliber Glock now in his hands. With my arm around his shoulder I lift him to his feet and we begin our journey back to the square. Despite a heavy limp Phil is keeping a good pace. I can hear a lot of movement behind us and turn to look. The two that managed to escape my attack are now regrouping and digging in the back seat of the truck.

Taking my GPS off my wrist and handing it to Phil, I scream at him, "Take it, run down this street and take a right onto the main road." I point at the entrance of the square. "As long as you have that GPS the good guys will be able to find you. Now go, stay hidden and don't ever come back here." Phil nods and pulls ahead of me. Slowing my pace, the two I left at the truck begin to open fire. I wait until Phil is well on his way and then turn to face my loose ends. Darting to my right I seek cover behind an alleyway and pull a fresh magazine and ready myself for the fight. Pulling my weapon into my shoulder I step out into the square and attack. Frozen, my eyes understand what is about to be and my M-4 drops ever so slightly. One of those waiting has shouldered a rocket propelled grenade (RPG) and I am dead in his sights.

The last thing my mind registers is the hiss of the grenade as it missiles towards me. It explodes at the far wall of the alley. My feet leave the ground and I am lost in the concussion somewhere between flying and falling as everything is stripped away. I collide hard into the wall and feel the slightest kiss of sand on my burning face. An iron taste of blood fills my mouth for a moment, only to be lost as I smash into the ground. On my back I struggle to breathe and see, but my vision is in soft focus. I push myself to stand and stumble up trying to find my rifle, but something is not right and I fall back into the warm earth. For the first time I see my leg, twisted and pouring blood. My boot is soaked red and I am wondering why I can't feel the wetness or notice the pain when I hear their voices.

My enemies are standing over me looking re-laxed and smiling. One has his rifle pointed at my face and I watch as his smile widens. The hard world is rushing back and everything is suddenly very clear. I look in the eye of the man who will end this and smile. It will be a good kill for him, a story to tell, maybe for the rest of his life. This is a soldier's death, my death. My body grows heavy and I am at peace as he takes aim.

Shots are fired and I watch as my enemies fall to the ground, their faces blank and dead. I don't un-derstand what is happening and battle to hold my eyes open. Shock is taking over. The bodies lie close and each has a symmetrical hole in their forehead. I know this handy work and try to see the source of the trajectory. Q and Marti are running side by side, Q with his scanning eye buried in his sight and Marti pulling out his med pack. The roar of a bird comes in close kicking up dirt and dust. It feels good against the burns on my face, but that is secondary to my weariness. I see Marti and Q hovering over me, going to work on the wounds. "You're going to be OK boss," Marti lies as he attempts to stop the bleeding.

Their voices fade and the world vanishes. I surrender to the darkness.

CHAPTER NINETEEN

I see blood in the rising tide of the evening as the water reaches my knees. In the sea of crimson are the faces of men, women and children. Only a few I recognize, but they all share one common characteristic, they are mute. I scan the scene, hands and arms thrash about as if trying to avoid drowning, but it is the faces covered in blood that reveal that their struggles are failing. Mouths open to gasp for a second more of life, but are quickly filled with the surrounding red water. The only sounds are hands franticly thrashing against the dark surface. It is strangely familiar as if a distant waterfall.

To my hips now, the pool's current draws me out into the dark horizon to join the bodies. I try to fight, but am overcome by the force. Each step out to sea is filled with the dread that I know so well. Soon I will be surrounded by them. The people around me glow maroon in the moonlight and realize my presence among them. I try to take hold of the panic in my heart and pace of my breathing, but terror engulfs me and my muscles flex hard for what is to come.

I make myself be still, so still a body glides over me, eyes closed in peace. The battle to survive is too strong and I begin to struggle against the current and boggy bottom refusing to become one of them. My battle awakes them from their sleep and in a sharp snap their faces come alive. Their black eyes open and turn to me in need. The first grabs my shoulder pulling me back into the blood. I surge forward only to find myself in the arms of another dragging me down and then another until their weight over-whelms me. I hammer them with my fists trying to smash my way to freedom, but each blow is met with another pair of hands grasping and yanking me into the deep swirling current.

My clenched fists are held submerged by the mass of bodies that swim and undulate like water moccasins. My body is in the hold of the many and their pressing grip stops any movement to escape. I surrender and they sense my weakness. The blood is up to my shoulders now as an arm slithers up my back through the base of my skull and wraps itself around my forehead forcing me to look up. Another slithers under my shirt sending a chill over my body as it slides up my chest finally latching a hold over my face so that between the two I can no longer turn my head. The blood has risen, fills my ears, and seeps into my mouth. I can taste the iron, but can do nothing except look into the massive night sky and take shallow breaths through my nose. I see the stars above and my mind reaches for their beauty away from this terror. Another hand slides up over my ear and clamps down on my nose with fingers spread over my eyes. I can't breathe and am only able to glimpse the sky through the graying fingers of my captors. Under the surface and in darkness , I struggle to stay alive, but their hold is too great. I am drowning.

A soft cry and I am awake. Confused, I gasp for air, drenched in sweat and trembling. Visions of the swirling dead and dying fade from my head as I try to get hold of this place. I see my wife on her side, sleeping, hands tucked under her cheek facing me, just like she always does and suddenly I find comfort. Another cry reminds me of my purpose and I begin the work of getting out of bed. My leg is stiff, but bears my weight. My ribs protest the disruption, loudly remembering an injury a lifetime ago. On my feet I take my first painful steps out of my bedroom. Every movement is accompanied by a pop or creak in a joint, but I don't mind. In the hallway I hear whimpers of distress and quicken my pace. Past a family photo from last Christmas I step over a snoring dog lost in visions. The whole house under a low sapphire moon is adrift in dreams, good dreams.

Despite the dark I know my way and turn into a baby blue bedroom and maneuver across a floor littered with bright red race cars, cowboys, and space men. A small boy sits up, waiting for his father to come. A last little sigh and I'm there sitting on the bed with my son. His hands reach out and I answer by pulling him into the cradle of my arms. It only takes a few timid breaths to find his peace. His body begins to surrender its tension; one last look into my eyes and he falls away into the night's stillness.

Even though I know he will probably sleep till morning, I linger a little longer just to make sure his nightmares don't return. Across the room his younger brother sleeps unaware. He is on his side just like his mother and I proudly see him grow bigger every day. In my arms the child's breathing ruffles. I look down into his big brown eyes unsure of the world until he finds me. In my arms, he nestles closer into my chest, "Shh my boy, don't be scared, I am here."

ABOUT THE AUTHORS

Manuel Carreon is a veteran of the Iraq and Afghanistan conflicts. He is a father of four, husband, son, musician, and writer. This is his first novel, but the second is soon to be completed. His self-help book on how to manage PTSD and your life after war will be available later this year.

Marla Dean, MA, Ph.D. is a playwright, professor of theatre, the Humanities and Creative Writing as well as a director for the stage. Currently, she teaches at Austin Community College and online for the University of Phoenix and Kaplan University. This is also her first novel, but not her last.